Totally Bound Publishing books by Haylynn Downing

The Cursed Rose
A Rose Among Beasts

The Cursed Rose

A ROSE AMONG BEASTS

HAYLYNN DOWNING

A Rose Among Beasts
ISBN # 978-1-80250-738-6
©Copyright Haylynn Downing 2024
Cover Art by Kelly Martin ©Copyright July 2024
Interior text design by Claire Siemaszkiewicz
Totally Bound Publishing

A ROSE AMONG BEASTS

Dedication

To Harley and Jen.
Thank you for supporting me in my creation,
exploration, and development in writing. Words
will never express my endless gratitude and love
for you both.

Chapter One

Brielle

Sobbing.

The noise wakes me from a dream, the haze of exhaustion still attempting to restrain me as I roll onto my side, my eyes parting just enough to make out the trembling figure hovering beside my bed.

"Sammy?" I whisper, my voice thick with sleep. "What's wrong? Did you have a bad dream?"

I reach over and turn on my bedside lamp, the bare bulb blinding, and wince as my pupils struggle to adjust to the sudden brightness.

"M-ma fe — own." Samuel whimpers, the thumb in his mouth warping his words past recognition. I scan him, taking in the pants of his favorite pajamas, a flannel decorated with multicolored trains, that cling to his legs. *He had an accident?*

"Ma fe own?" I repeat his words, gritting my teeth as frustration blooms in my chest. It's nearly impossible to understand him when he speaks like this, but now is not the time to scold him for a habit he picked up in his infancy. With a rushed breath, I rerun his words through my head, piecing together the broken sentence until it clicks. *Mama fell down.*

"Shit." I move, scooping my little brother into my arms, and race with him down the hall toward the back of the house, panic churning my stomach.

Our mother is currently undergoing chemotherapy for a brain tumor they discovered shortly after Samuel's dramatic arrival into the world. The radiation treatment leaves her weak and lethargic, but the tumor it's targeting can cause dizziness, fainting spells and seizures. Which one is the reason she fell?

"Mom?" I'm unable to keep the panic from my voice as I spot her, crumpled in an unconscious heap on the carpeted floor by her bed. "Mom...?" I kneel beside her, the scent of vomit assaulting my nose as I set Sammy on his feet and grasp her wrist, squeezing until I can feel her weak pulse drum unsteadily against my hand. *She's alive.* "Mom, can you hear me?"

I release her wrist and reach across her body to grab the opposite arm, gently pulling it until she rolls limply onto her back. Her face and clothes are covered in last night's chicken broth—the only food she can manage to keep down—and her forehead is bleeding as if she struck something when she fell. *Dammit, where is Dad?* I scan the dark room, my eyes jumping from his untouched side of the bed to the work boots thrown haphazardly in front of the closet door. Did he just get home?

"Dad, help!" I glance over my shoulder, praying to see him peering around a corner, or running to our rescue, but he isn't. The house behind us is dark and empty. "Dad?"

There's no response, no call from his distant voice, telling me that he's coming. *We're on our own.* My head reels at the realization, the air leaving my lungs as panic constricts them so tightly I feel, for a moment, like I'm suffocating.

Samuel's small hand tugs on my shirt and his quiet sobs ground me enough for a shaky breath to sneak in through my parted lips. "It's okay. She's going to be fine."

I force the lie past the lump that's beginning to form in my throat, but even as I say it, I'm unsure if I'm trying to comfort Sammy or myself. Shaking, I stand and turn toward the nightstand, where the landline is waiting on the charger. I snatch it, and quickly kneel back down, tucking Samuel against my chest as I dial the three numbers I've always dreaded needing to use.

"Nine-one-one, what's your emergency?" a female voice, strong and certain, crackles over the line.

"It's my mom, I need an ambulance!" I rattle off our address, trying my best to remain calm as I answer the throng of questions she quickly spews over the static. She ensures me that help is on the way, but her promise does nothing to soothe my nerves as I drop my hand back to my mother's fragile wrist and count out the unsteady beats of her pulse. The operator can say anything she wants…it won't change the reality of the situation unfolding in front of me. *My mother is dying.*

"The paramedics are almost there, sweetheart. I need you to open the door for them." The woman's voice snaps me out of my trance, and in the distance, I can hear the faint sound of a siren growing louder.

"I—I can't leave her." My objection is weak, and it's nearly impossible to keep the tears stinging my eyes from spilling over.

"They can't help her if they can't get inside. You're almost done," she counters, another promise she should know better than to make. *This won't end until…*

"Fire truck?" Samuel mumbles around his thumb, his curls brushing my chin as he looks hopefully toward the red lights flashing outside of the bedroom window. I need to move, but my legs are still cemented to the floor underneath me, my fingers wound tightly around my mother's cooling skin. *I'll only be gone for a few seconds.*

"Just a few seconds," I whisper, forcing myself to move. With the phone to my ear and Samuel in my arms, I run to the front door and slip the lock out of place, yanking on the heavy metal until it slides soundlessly open. "She's in here, please hurry!"

The night is cold, the chill in the air causing goosebumps as men rush up the sidewalk, following my instructions as I numbly direct them down the hallway.

Strangers. I'm leaving her in the hands of strangers.

I drop the phone, uncaring as the plastic splinters at my feet, and move to follow them, stopped only by a large hand that is quick to clasp my shoulder.

"We should give them some room to work." When I look back, an officer, dressed in a navy uniform so dark it leaves him one with the night, is standing behind me, a solemn look on his face.

"She needs me, I have to—" My sentence breaks as the paramedic, who should be inside saving my mother, appears beside me, the quick shake of his head shattering my heart.

Dead. She's dead?

The officer's face softens with sympathy as he watches the recognition ring across my features, the hand on my shoulder tightening as I sway unsteadily on my feet. "I'm sorry. Why don't you come and have a seat in my car?"

"N-no...I—I was only gone for a few seconds..." I whisper, unable to wrap my head around the reality attempting to drown me. A loud sob rips from my throat, and I sway again, my knees buckling beneath me. I crumple. "It was just a few *seconds*."

The officer kneels beside me, his arms wrapping around my shoulders as if he's afraid that I'll collapse further in on myself, while the paramedic begins to lift Samuel out of my arms.

Screaming. Who's screaming?

My eyes jump to Samuel, but his lips are pressed into a tight line, his large eyes full of fear as he stares back at me, mortified. It's me. I'm screaming.

My chest is tight—too tight—as the officer helps me to my feet. I can't breathe, can't think. I'm panicking, my breath coming in uneven, rasped breaths that make my head spin. I bend forward, bile rushing up my throat as my dinner spills from my lips, the food slapping unpleasantly against the deck as I heave uncontrollably. I can't *breathe.*

Why did I leave her alone? This is my fault.

My fault.

My fault.

My fault.

My fault.

I blink and draw in a sharp breath as the memory recedes, leaving a large ache in its wake that has me shivering, despite the warmth of the city bus. I pull my thin jacket tighter around me, and clutch my resume to my chest as thunder crackles overhead, rattling the roof of the bus. It's raining, storm clouds darkening the already black sky, and the wind shakes the bus so violently that it jostles on its wheels. *Maybe it'll lighten up before my stop?*

Thunder claps overhead, taunting me as the storm rages on just past my window, rain pelting the glass as sheets pour down from the sky. It's late, the bus all but devoid of passengers as we head toward the last stop of the night, those that remain onboard grumbling to themselves about the horrible weather. *A shitty ending to a shitty day.*

My breath fogs the glass as I run my hands along my legs, trying to work out some of the soreness that lingers deep within the muscles. On my way into the city this morning, the promise of going home with a job at the end of the day sweetened the journey, distracting my mind from the pain of walking all those miles in shoes that stopped fitting a few years ago. Now, with no job to keep the negativity at bay, I can't stop my mind from replaying old choices and cursing the way that my life is turning out.

"Last stop, everyone off," the driver calls. He shoves the door open and the rain-scented air swarms in, the fresh scent masking the musky odor of the large cabin. Men and women grunt as they shuffle toward the front of the bus, and I stand, pulling my purse over my shoulder and tucking my resume beneath my jacket. As I step toward the door, I pull up my hood and scan the bus stop outside, momentarily contemplating camping out until the rain lightens until I see the homeless man and his heroin pipe already taking up residence on the bench. His grimy smile finds me as I jump off the last step, my nerves sparking to life as I dash down the street with my chin to my chest. I'm soaked before I'm halfway down the block, my shoes squelching with the water they're drowning in as the wind whips around me, a frigid blast that weaves through the fibers of my clothing until my teeth chatter uncontrollably. I don't slow down. Not until my house comes into view.

It's small, a single-story with two bedrooms, one bath, and a muddy, unfenced backyard. The siding is faded, an ugly grayish hue that leads me to believe it was once painted to match the sky, and the gutters hang lopsided and crooked along the roof. I run up the cement steps, and pull open the rusted door, my fingers fumbling for the light switch as I step through the threshold. *It's not my home...and it never will be.*

I pull off my socks and shoes, and peel out of my soaked jacket, frowning down at the ruined sheet of paper still pressed against my chest.

"What a fucking waste," I mutter, crumpling it and dropping it to the floor with my other soaked items.

Stifling a yawn, I shuffle down the hall into the kitchen, moving quietly as I pull open the fridge to retrieve a bottle of water and the lunch meat. I tiptoe around the small space, all too aware of Samuel asleep in the next room, and make myself a sandwich before I plop down at the dining room table to eat.

"Brielle, is that you?" a groggy voice calls. I pause mid-bite and watch as my father walks into the room scratching at his chin, his gray hair appearing greasy in the white kitchen light. "How did your working interview at the hospital go?"

I try to conceal my frown as I take a sip of water, unsure of how I'm going to respond. Dad has been working his ass off trying to support us since Mom died six years ago, leaving a mountain of debt in her wake. He works such long hours at the warehouse that there are days I won't even see him in passing. How am I supposed to tell him that he's still stuck being the sole provider for our family? "I made enough to cover our next grocery bill."

"Don't stall, Bri," he scolds, pulling out the chair beside me and sitting down. A thick brow raises above his hazel eyes, and I sigh, chewing on the inside of my cheek.

"I...didn't get the job," I murmur, biting into my sandwich as his relaxed face scrunches into a scowl.

"I thought your professors said you were a shoo-in for the position? Didn't the formal interview go well?" The accusation lingering beneath his question makes me flinch.

"The formal interview went great, and so did the working interview today, I just—"

"You just what? I don't understand what happened."

"I just didn't get selected! There were other candidates there that had more schooling, training, and work experience than I do. There are more nursing students than there are jobs right now. I'm sorry."

My words settle in the silent room, my face heated with embarrassment as an unidentifiable emotion filters across my father's face. *I didn't do enough.* Dad is doing everything he can to keep us afloat, and I can't even manage to get a job.

My father rubs the back of his neck, his other hand reaching out to clasp mine. "I'm sorry, Bri, I shouldn't have yelled. I'm just tired. Work's been forcing a lot of overtime on us, and I haven't been getting enough sleep."

"It's okay," I mumble, forcing a smile to my lips as I pull my hand away from his. I gesture toward the hall, feigning a yawn as I stretch. "You should get back to bed, I'm about to call it a night anyway. I want to make sure that I'm at the library first thing tomorrow morning so I can search for more job postings."

"Atta girl, you'll get the next one, just wait. Goodnight, honey." He pushes himself up and away from the table, yawning as he leaves.

I watch him go, no longer hungry enough to finish eating. Standing, I grab a paper towel and wrap my sandwich with it, placing it in the fridge for later before heading down the hall toward the bathroom. I shut the door behind me, peel off my scrubs, and hang them over the bathtub before turning to face the mirror above the sink. My exhausted reflection stares back at me, the bags underneath my eyes aging me well past my twenty-four years, their normally hazel color bloodshot and red-rimmed from the lack of sleep. The lighting above me washes out my pale complexion, but the freckles sprinkled across my cheeks and nose are still dark, despite the lack of sunlight I've been getting. I guess I'd consider myself pretty if I cared at all about the way that I looked.

I shrug, and pull my light brown waves into a messy bun at the top of my head, turning on the cold water and using it to wash my face. I brush my teeth, pee, and get dressed into the oversized T-shirt and shorts I keep stashed underneath the sink before heading back out to the living room.

When we first moved here after Mom died, Dad tried to convince me to share the master bedroom with Samuel. I know he felt bad about the downgrade in our living situation, but Sammy was still a toddler—taking naps throughout the day and going to bed early in the evening—so I opted to sleep in the living room to keep from throwing off his sleep schedule. It was a rough adjustment period for me, learning to live without a mother or any privacy, but I managed. It's been so many years at this point that I've almost forgotten what it feels like to stretch out on a mattress. *Almost.*

Bending down, I grab my quilt and pillow from the box underneath the side table and drop onto the couch, exhausted. I roll onto my side, facing away from the room, and close my heavy eyes, leaning into the fatigue that quickly advances on me. I know I should be planning, thinking of the next steps I'll need to take to try to secure my future, but my thoughts are too jumbled, my pillow too comfortable. After such a long day, I'm powerless and far too willing to succumb to the sleep that quickly takes me.

Chapter Two

Xander

My chair legs scrape against the wooden floor as I stand, the movement causing an audible gulp to echo from the man sitting across from me. I bury my amusement, keeping my face impassive as I round my desk, sipping from the glass of whiskey I'd been enjoying before my brothers interrupted me with this fucker.

"Lincoln Fisher, right?" It's a rhetorical question — unfortunately for him, I know who he is. "I'm assuming you know who *we* are."

He bristles at my statement, shifting in his chair as his eyes dart between me and the two men hovering on either side of him. *My brothers.* Two men bound to me by nothing more than the last name, but who I'd give anything, including my life, to protect.

"I know who you are," he mutters. His voice is steady despite his current situation, but the sweat beginning to bead on his forehead betrays his calm façade. *He's scared.*

"That's great, because I think formalities would be a fucking waste given the circumstances." His eyes widen as I pull my revolver from the breast pocket of my suit jacket, the flash of metal sending him scrambling to his feet. Everett, the oldest in our little 'family', is quick to grab the small man by his shoulders, slamming him back into the seat so forcefully that the wooden frame cracks amidst the struggle. I can't keep the grin off my face, tipping my head back to finish off my whiskey as Lincoln's pathetic pleas begin filling the room, his composure snapping.

"L-let me go, please!" His voice breaks as his body begins to shake, his struggles useless against the hands keeping him trapped in his chair. Everett doesn't waver, his thick frame easily overpowering Lincoln's scrawny, out-of-shape build, his face expressionless as the man continues to beg him for his life.

"You're trying to barter with the wrong brother, Lincoln." My voice cuts through his pointless blubbering, his throat contracting as he swallows and returns his attention to me. "Let's play a game."

I set my empty glass on the desk and flick open the cylinder of my revolver, holding it up to reveal the single bullet waiting in the chamber. I snap it shut and spin it, losing track of the bullet as I lean against the desk, waiting until it's stopped to pull down the hammer.

"I want to know which gang you report to and how many other members of your crew are stashed within our facilities. If you tell me, I'll *think* about forgiving the money that you stole from us, and let you out of here alive. Refuse, and we'll start playing."

I think for a moment that Lincoln might faint. His skin turns a sickly white as I turn the barrel of the gun on him, and his body begins to slump forward in his chair.

"Tapping out so soon, Linc? We haven't even started yet!" Rhys jeers, a laugh rippling from his chest. I raise a brow in his direction, silently warning him to remember his place as he grabs at the limp man's clothes.

The youngest of our group, it's not Rhys' looks that betray his age, but his mouth. His quick tongue and dark humor convey his immaturity to those around him, which could put a target on his back, in a business like ours. He gives me a curt nod in understanding and presses his lips together as he forces Lincoln back into an upright position, the man's sweat rolling in waves down his face.

"Come on, man," Lincoln whines. He's pulling his hands through his hair, his shoulders hunching as he shrugs out of Rhys' grasp. "I'm not, I mean, I was but— God, please don't kill me."

I let out a loud sigh, making my annoyance evident as he continues talking, my patience growing thinner with each word that leaves his lips. Without warning, I snap my hand forward, smashing the gun into his nose, crushing the bone, and causing a loud howl to erupt from his throat. He shrinks back into the chair, cupping his nose as blood begins running down his face, splattering a dark crimson stain onto his gray slacks. More money lost to this piece of shit. *I should've had them pick him up* after *his shift.* I groan, rolling my eyes as more blood drips onto his pants and vest, ruining the expensive fabric. The suit he's wearing is a uniform we have custom tailored for the dealers of our high roller tables, an expense that I *normally* believe is worth the cost, but am currently cursing myself over. "Quit your fucking rambling. I want answers, and I want them now."

"All right, all right! Listen, I—I don't want any trouble. I left The Wolves a few months ago. I just used them for a quick hook-up here and there, but I'm trying to get clean. I got myself a job, and I haven't been late or missed a single shift until today." His eyes jump again to my brothers, as if blaming them for his tarnished attendance record. He wouldn't be here if he hadn't crossed us, and that's a point I'll be sure to make clear. "The stolen chips were a mistake, but it wasn't my fault, I swear."

The admission to previously working with The Wolves, a lower-level gang full of wannabe mobsters, isn't news to me. While Rhys and Everett were out collecting our *guest*, I tracked down every ounce of available information I could find on him, and his affiliation with that gang is only a pebble in comparison to the mountain of other trash I'd found on this prick. Mixed in with useless information about a shitty childhood growing up in the system, I found prior arrest records for theft, vandalism, possession of a controlled substance, and sexual assault. All the charges were dropped before he was ever processed, so the fucker never saw the inside of a jail cell. I don't believe for one second that he cut ties with the gang that pulled him off the streets, but this renewed citizen act of his has piqued my curiosity.

"It's this guy, George Beaumont...he's been harassing the staff for weeks. I caught him stealing chips from another table, and reported him to my manager. When I saw he was back in the casino last night, I went to find security, but by the time I'd returned to my table, he'd already disappeared with my stash of chips." Lincoln's voice is rough with congestion, his eyes already swelling and bruising. He's watching me as if he believes that his words should be enough to placate me, but he seems to have forgotten that we're still out twenty grand because of *him* and his stupidity.

"As of tonight, you're no longer our employee. I'll be looking into the information that you've provided, and if I find out that you've been lying to me, I will track you down, and you will *wish* that I'd killed you. Do you understand?" I lean down, lock my hands onto the arms of his chair, and allow my size to reinforce the threat. He's smart enough to realize at this point that I prefer him silent, so his lips remain sealed as he nods his agreement. I shove away from him, and the chair leg snaps after the evening of abuse it's endured, sending the man crashing to the floor with a *thud*. I replace my revolver in my jacket, grab my cell, and stalk toward the office door, a new target in sight. "We'll be in touch, Lincoln."

I leave my brothers to deal with him, fuming with a wave of anger I know becomes dangerous if not extinguished. *Who the hell is hiring these people?* I should've never delegated my workload, the casino now taking an unnecessary blow that leaves us out twenty *fucking* grand, and mixed in with a group that thrives on violence. *Fuck today!*

I head toward the bank of elevators at the end of the hall, trying to ignore the blood boiling a path through my veins. As much as I'd like to march back into that office and smash Lincoln's skull in, I know that I can't kill him. Not yet, at least. I need him alive if he's going to lead me to his employer, and although I know his affiliation with The Wolves isn't a farce, I can't help but feel that there's more to this charade of his.

I dial my informant's number as I wait for the elevator car to climb the forty-four floors to me, rolling my neck in an attempt to release some of the stress trapped within the muscles there.

"Beast? D'you not get the files I sent over?" *Beast.* A nickname bestowed upon me by my father to be used by men who either respect or fear me. My informant has made it clear which side of the fence he sits on. David, a hacker that's been with our company since I was a child, is an older gentleman who, despite his age, keeps up to date on the latest technology to ensure he never disappoints.

"I got them. I need information on a Mr. George Beaumont, now. Criminal records, work history, I want to know where he lives, and how he takes his coffee in the morning. You can send the files to my email, I want them by eight." I bark the order into my phone as the elevator doors slide open, and end the call before he can respond.

As I step into the elevator, I transfer an extra ten thousand into his bank account and descend to the lower garage. The twenty grand stolen from us is hardly enough to concern ourselves with, but we have an image to protect, and the Grimm Brothers don't take kindly to thievery. *Let's see what we can dig up on Beaumont.* If he turns out to be another crew member of The Wolves, then we *might* just have a bigger problem on our hands than a suicidal man idiotic enough to fuck with the wrong family.

The elevator doors open, and I step out into the private garage, nodding at the security guard who tosses me the keys to my ride. It's a newer sports car, the black leather interior a perfect match to the dark exterior paint, with windows tinted enough that I could fuck someone against the glass and a passerby would be none the wiser.

I get in, the engine purring as I put it in drive and start toward the exit, the gates lifting so I can tear out onto the wet pavement. It's late, and although our office is in the heart of downtown, the roads are nearly empty at this time of night. I try to resist the urge to check the time, but the clock displayed on my dashboard lures me in like a moth to the flame. Knowing the time won't change the list of things that have to be done once I get home, and will only prove to stress me further, but I'm a self-destructive bastard with no self-control, so I check anyway. *Twelve-thirty-two.* I've got less than eight hours until those files are in my email, which means I have even less time to plan. What if I find out that Beaumont *is* a member of The Wolves? They've never caused any problems for us before, but am I supposed to believe that they're knocking on our door because they're a little strapped for cash? *No one is that fucking stupid.*

I pinch the bridge of my nose, the beginnings of a headache pounding through the front of my skull as I navigate home on autopilot. I'm so distracted by my thoughts that I don't realize I've made it home until the faint beeping of the garage door unlocking brings me back. *I need to be more careful.* I'll be damned if it's a car wreck that kills me after surviving the fucking life I've had.

The lock clicks shut behind me as our automated alarm system whirls to life, and I cross through the empty house that I share with my brothers, my footsteps against the stone flooring the only noise reverberating through the large home. I pass from the foyer into the living room, an open space with expansive windows, French doors, and two leather sofas. Our dining room and kitchen are separated only by a steel beam that spans the length of the ceiling, and as I turn right down the back hall, I realize, once again, how large our house truly is. Unnecessarily large. I pass a theater room, the basement, a few spare guest rooms, and an additional bath before I enter the last room in this hallway. It's a home gym, a space that we keep stocked with the latest and greatest workout equipment, and mirrors so that we're always able to check our form.

Stalking forward, I peel off my suit jacket and shirt, tossing them both over a nearby bench as I kick off my shoes. I'm eyeing the heavy bag hanging in a corner across the room, and although I know I should tape my knuckles first, I'm unwilling to waste the time to do so.

George Beaumont.

I cross the room, my right fist swinging and connecting with the bag so forcefully that it swings backward enough to collide with the wall. My left fist is quick to follow through, the bag absorbing the blows and jostling on its chain as I move. I keep swinging. How long have they been stealing from under my fucking nose? *Worthless, disappointing Beast.* I push harder, my hands going numb and my knuckles splitting open, but I keep going. Blood splatters the bag, but still, I don't stop. Not until my father's voice is gone.

Breathless, I throw one last punch then turn away from the bag to find Everett watching me. He's hovering in the doorway, his brown eyes locked on my bloodied fists.

"What the fuck are you doing?" I bark. My voice is venomous, my anger refueled by the concern I can see lingering in his gaze.

"Lincoln shouldn't be causing any more problems," he states, easily ignoring my outburst. After living with me for so long, I'm sure he's become immune to my snappy remarks and hateful words. His brow tips up, a silent question in his gaze, but I refuse to unload the thoughts plaguing my mind onto his shoulders.

"Great. Thanks." I can't stop myself from being short with him, moving forward to snatch my discarded clothes and shoes. "I've got work to do. If you need me, I'll be in my study."

I shove past him, ignoring the guilt attempting to smash its way to the surface, and instead choose to focus on my need for answers. I pass Rhys, who's flipping mindlessly through TV channels in the living room, and do my best to ignore his gaze as it follows me up the stairs.

David is going to be sending the information on Beaumont in a few hours, but I need to see what, if anything, I can dig up on my own first. If I'm lucky, maybe I'll find something tying him to The Wolves so I can kick down his front door first thing in the morning. I'd like to put an end to this little game before it's had the chance to begin.

I let out an irritated groan, sitting at my desk and pulling my hair free of the tie holding it back in a ponytail. I rub at my temples, trying to ease the pressure building within my skull, and turn on my computer, watching as it slowly blinks to life. The clock fills the screen as it loads, its large numbers taunting me as they flash and disappear into the background. *One-fifty-seven.*

Six hours, Beaumont, and I'm coming for you.

Chapter Three

Brielle

"What time did you get home last night, Bri?" Samuel's question floats to me from the kitchen, where I left him to finish his breakfast—a plate of scrambled eggs drenched in ketchup and burnt toast smothered in enough butter to clog his young arteries.

He'd woken up before me this morning and, in an attempt to let me sleep, tried cooking breakfast on his own. I woke to the smell of burning food, the plume of smoke coming from the toaster thick enough to make me believe our house was on fire, that initial rush of adrenaline still making my knees wobble. After realizing what had happened, and rescuing the bread from the toaster, I did my best to salvage the eggs by sprinkling salt, pepper and shredded cheese on them until they were edible again. Coating them in ketchup was Sammy's idea, something he said he'd learned from his friend and insisted was the *best* way to eat them.

"It was late," I shout my reply, my mouth full of toothpaste as I scrub feverishly at my tongue. I'd hoped that the minty flavor would be enough to overpower the lingering aftertaste the toast left behind, but, so far, my efforts have been in vain. I'd tried to throw it out, the edges so charred they crumbled when I touched them, but Samuel refused to let me, drenching his pieces in butter, and shoving them into his mouth before I could take them from him. He just wanted to help, I know. He believes, after growing up around my father, that any wasted food is wasted money, but some things are *beyond* saving. I couldn't be mad at him for doing something that he thought was best for our struggling family, so instead of arguing with him, I joined him, hoping the butter would camouflage the burnt flavor. *It didn't.*

I spit, rinse my brush, and head back into the kitchen, the ripped skinny jeans I'd thrown on pinching uncomfortably into my thighs as I walk. Just like my shoes, my wardrobe consists of clothing that's either too small or so old that it's falling apart, my need for new clothes low on my father's list of priorities. "What time did you go to bed?"

"Late." I round the corner into the kitchen, watching as a mischievous grin breaks out on Sammy's face. I scowl at him, earning a light laugh as he pushes himself away from the table to place his plate in the sink.

"You need to shower and get your room picked up today, okay? I've gotta get to the library. Stay away from the appliances while I'm gone, got it?" I point at the stove and toaster, guilt prickling through my chest as his smile quickly evaporates.

"Do you have to go?" He's quiet, shifting from one foot to the other, his hands fidgeting with the stencil peeling off of his gym shorts. It's Saturday, a day we'd normally get to spend together, our weekdays too consumed by school and chores, but now, without a job, I have to spend every free second looking for another work opportunity.

"I'm sorry, Sammy... Did you want to come with me?" I wait, watching him as he shakes his head, his brown curls bouncing from the movement. "I'll come home around lunchtime, okay? Dad had to cover a morning shift, but he should be back soon."

I give him a quick hug, squeezing him until he starts to giggle, the sound of his breathless laughs still ringing in my ears as I walk down the sidewalk toward town. It's cold, the autumn breeze whips my hair around my face, and I curse myself for forgetting a jacket. After everything that happened this morning, I was running late and didn't stop to think of what the weather might be like before rushing out of the door. *At least it isn't raining.*

I groan and rub my frozen hands up and down my arms, silently cursing the sun for only taking the edge off the bitter wind. I tuck my chin and stretch my legs, forcing myself to take longer strides until I reach the edge of town, my quick breaths clouding in front of me. I pass the coffee shop, a bar, a liquor store and an abandoned church before I turn down an alleyway to cut through to the library. I sigh with relief when I cross through its front entrance, the wave of heat working to melt my cold and stiff muscles.

"Good morning, Brielle. What're you doing back so soon?" I turn toward the warm voice and easily spot the librarian, Mrs. Warner, perched in her seat behind the counter. She's an older woman, with glasses that slide low over her nose and shoulders that are rounded from years of slouching, her gray curls pinned to the back of her head in a fifties-style updo.

"Good morning. I just came to use one of the computers again. Should I sign in?" I walk toward the counter, unable to contain the smile that creeps onto my face. The smell of books and the quiet offered by libraries have always been a welcome distraction for me when I've been desperate for an escape, and they work now, calming my fears.

"You know, dear, I seem to have misplaced that sheet this morning. Why don't you get started, and when I find it, I'll sign you in myself." Her wrinkled lips return my smile, a knowing gleam lighting up her eyes as her fragile fingers push her glasses back into place.

"Thank you." I turn toward the back wall and the table of computers that line it, surprised to see that all of them are unoccupied. It looks like, despite the late start, I've still managed to be the first one in today, the rest of the building is deserted and empty.

I cross the room and sit at the computer in front of the single window, the blinds rolled up to let in the early morning sunlight. I wave the mouse, waiting until the screen has popped to life to type in my username and password. The internet browser loads as soon as I'm logged in, and I pull up a job search website, sighing as I begin scrolling through the short list of recommended postings. *Let's see what I can find today.*

* * * *

At noon, I log off the computer, my eyes sore and my heart heavy. In the few job postings I'd managed to find, I'd been discouraged by their requirements for previous work history, and the notated remarks stating any resume submitted without would be discarded and overlooked. In the end, after scouring for hours, I'd ignored their warnings and prayed that by attaching my college transcript, I'd snag enough attention to at least earn an interview with their practice.

Standing, I walk back up toward the front counter, maneuvering around a mother herding her children toward the front door, and stop at the counter, watching as Mrs. Warner juggles a large stack of books in her unsteady hands.

"All finished?" She sets the stack down and turns toward me, a dramatic breath huffing past her lips, before she seems to remember something, and slips off her stool. "Oh, Brielle! Let me grab that document you printed."

She grabs a piece of paper off the printer behind her and slides it across the counter toward me, along with the previously missing sign-in sheet for the computers. "Thank you. How much do I owe you?"

I open my purse, reaching in to search for my wallet when Mrs. Warner's hand lands on my own, her gentle squeeze stealing my attention away from my bag.

"Don't you worry about it, just focus on getting that job, all right?" She winks, nodding toward the resume laid down in front of me.

"Mrs. Warner, I can't—"

She waves her hand, dismissing my objection as an older gentleman approaches the counter, her attention rotating to assist him. *Thank you...*

I pick up my resume, clutching the thin piece of paper to my chest, and pick up the pen to sign out. I scrawl my signature across the sheet, *Brielle Beaumont*, and turn toward the front door, feeling lighter as I step into the warming afternoon. I keep my chin tilted toward the sky as I head home, relishing in the warmth that spreads across my cheeks, knowing that within the next month, the temperatures will drop so much that we'll be hunkered inside trying to stay warm. *I'll need to go through our winter clothes soon to see what Samuel can still fit into.*

I'm careful to watch my step, the sidewalk beneath me crumbling in some places, the deterioration of the cement almost unnoticed when compared to the rusted vehicles and buildings of this town. It's no secret that the people who live here are impoverished. The small population and growing crime rate of our area tends to leave the county to donate any money to projects happening within city limits. What little money we do receive from the government is always divided between the school and the library; the families with children hoping that by sacrificing paved roads and updated buildings, their children might be able to find a way out before it's too late.

That's why I need this job.

I feel guilty as soon as the thought crosses my mind, the reality of my situation crushing the longing my heart has for a life of my own. I want so much more for myself than this but...how could I ever leave? The detrimental financial situation my family is in was only made worse when I decided to go to college. My father refused to let me take out any student loans, and instead, paid for my schooling out of his pocket. All the money that he spent on me could have been put toward our mother's old medical bills, which collect interest and grow over time. I can't ever leave them, not until I can get them out of this town, and I can't do that without money. *What am I going to do?*

Suddenly, I'm falling, my foot caught on an uneven crack in the sidewalk, my resume flying from my hands as I crash to the ground. *Fuck!* I land on my hands and knees, the skin scraping away as they connect with the cement, tears springing to my eyes as my face heats with embarrassment. "Dammit."

"Brielle!" I hear Samuel's shout before I see him. *What is he doing?* He knows better than to be out here alone. I push myself onto my knees, looking up as Samuel rounds our street corner, his chest and feet bare, his curls soaking wet.

"Samuel? What're you —"

"It's Dad!" His frantic reply cuts me off, his red face blurring and morphing until he's a toddler again, my breath catching as I'm momentarily thrown six years back in time. "We have to hurry!"

He's in front of me now, his hands wrapped around my upper arm as he tries to pull me to my feet. "What? What happened?"

I swallow my rising panic, refusing to let myself disappear into the past when I'm so very needed in the present.

"I don't know! These two big guys came to the house looking for him. I think one of them has a gun. We have to warn him before he gets hurt!" He rushes out an explanation that leaves my head spinning, his hands tugging at me until I'm back on my feet. *This can't be happening.* I have to be dreaming. People don't watch their mothers die, only to have their fathers ripped away from them, too. "Brielle, come on!"

I follow him, a limp in my step as we run down the sidewalk, our feet thundering against the walkway beneath them. When we're a few houses away from our own, I pull Samuel to a stop beside me, hushing his protests as my eyes scan the surrounding area. It's not hard to spot the black SUV that's parked in the street, its shiny new exterior a beacon amidst the sea of broken down and rusted lemons that surround it. *They must be from the city.* No one in our town can afford a car like this, and even if they could, I would have seen it before.

No, these are outsiders…so what do they want with our father? "Follow me."

I pull Samuel's hand, running down the side of our neighbor's home and into the wooded area that borders our neighborhood, hoping that it'll be enough to hide us.

"Bri—" I wave my hand, silencing Samuel's protest as I motion for him to stay quiet, tugging him along as we begin the trek toward our backyard. It's muddy, yesterday's rainstorm having turned the earth into a slick sludge that encases our feet and slows our pace, a thick coverage of thorn bushes snagging into our flesh as we go. Samuel doesn't complain, not when the branches cut his chest, and not when I shove him to the ground behind a large tree, my attention locked on the silhouette standing at our backdoor. It's a man, his large back pressed against the glass as if he's casually waiting for someone to come home, his relaxed appearance only refuted by the gun clutched in his hand. *What the fuck am I supposed to do?*

I take my purse off my shoulder and drop it to the ground, rooting through it until I find the can of pepper spray my father bought me when I'd started taking night courses. I open it, hovering my finger over the trigger as I look down at my little brother, a child, who I've all but raised on my own. He's bleeding in some places, his bare feet and sweatpants coated in mud, but he's safe. Alive. If I could, I'd send him to our neighbor's house to call for help, but the police stopped making runs here years ago. *We're on our own.*

"Stay here, Samuel. Do not come inside, no matter what you hear, do you understand? Someone will come to get you when it's safe." He nods his understanding, hunkering lower in the brush, his brown locks blending seamlessly with the branches that surround him. I peer around the tree again, watching as the man disappears further into the house, providing the opportunity that I need. *It's now, or never.*

Pushing myself up, I dash toward the back of the house, flattening myself against the vinyl siding as I inch my way toward the glass door. I can hear murmured voices coming from inside, but it's impossible to decipher what they're saying. Tightening my grip on the pepper spray, I reach out and grab the handle of the door, yank it open and jump into the doorway.

At first, I think that I've caught them by surprise, the brunet sitting on our couch staring at me in something akin to shock, or awe, but a gun pressing against my temple quickly extinguishes the thought.

"Drop it." The order comes from the man wielding the weapon, his face blocked from my view by the barrel cooling my skin. He's a lot bigger up close, the expensive suit he's wearing doing nothing to conceal the mass of muscle he has packed onto his body. "I said drop it!"

I glance down at my hand, at the only form of protection I have against these men, and weigh my options. If I hit him, I might be able to duck the shot, grab the phone, and get to the bathroom so I can call Dad and warn him. If not...

"I'd do as he says, pet." The brunet pushes himself up off the couch slowly, as if moving too fast will somehow set off the gun that's held against my skull. *Maybe not the gun...but the man.*

I eye the metal again, chewing on my lower lip, and release my fingers, allowing the aluminum can to clatter against the linoleum floor.

A low laugh emits from the man beside me, and the gun finally drops, bringing the man into view. I almost stumble away from him, an unfamiliar feeling coiling in the pit of my stomach as I stare up at him, bewitched. He's smirking, a devilish grin pulling at the corner of his lips as his cold blue eyes tear me apart. He's... beautiful.

"Good girl." His praise sends a shiver through my body, leaving me unprepared for the hand that latches onto my upper arm to pull me further into the house. "Now, who the hell are you?"

Chapter Four

Xander

"I came to warn my father." Her response surprises me, and nothing *ever* surprises me. After hours of research last night, and skimming what files David had sent me this morning, I'd had no idea that George had a kid. *If you can even call her that.* The woman standing in front of me is anything but a child, the curves of her body enough to make my mouth water with desire. "Let me go."

A scowl mars her pretty face, and I can't help the irritation that rises from her demand, the confidence she's showing striking a nerve of mine that few are able to reach. "Where *is* your father, Princess? I'd like to know where the man that's been stealing from me —"

"You've got the wrong house. My father isn't a thief...and my name is *Brielle*." She interrupts, her face flushing as she corrects me.

Everett doesn't attempt to hide the snicker that leaves him, his eyes unapologetically meeting mine before they return to the small woman struggling in my grasp.

"Interrupting me and pissing me off isn't going to earn your father my favor." I don't attempt to keep the growl from my voice, her lack of fear only aiding the anger already burning through my chest. "I'm only going to ask you one more fucking time. Where is he?"

She scoffs, a resolve settling on her face as she stares up at me, unbreaking and accepting. *She's willing to die for him.* I curse, fed up with her games, but she doesn't flinch, her eyes moving between Everett and me as she waits, patiently, for one of us to make the next move.

"Have it your way, Princess," I mutter, releasing her arm and shoving her forward. She stumbles, her bloodied knees giving out, but Everett moves fast enough to keep her from hitting the floor, his arms quick to steady her. "If you won't let your father answer for his actions, then you'll have to answer for them yourself. Get her to the fucking car."

Everett only hesitates for a moment, his light features darkening as he moves to follow my command. He secures an arm around Brielle's waist and begins to tug her toward the front door, oblivious as she begins to struggle in his hold.

"Wait. Wait! My father hasn't stolen anything. You're wrong!" She's seething, her face heating with untamed emotions as she flails, her balled-up fists smacking against the arm secured around her waist.

"Wrong?" I hold up a hand, signaling for Everett to wait, and slowly inch forward to pick up the duffel bag we'd discovered in George's closet. I unzip the bag and tip it forward enough to showcase the colorful array of poker chips stashed within it, the black canvas filled to the brim. Her face falls as she scans them, her eyes racing over the insignia engraved on each chip and confusion furrows her brows. Not only are there more chips than I'd been expecting to find, but plopped on top like a fucking cherry on a goddamn sundae, is a note, with the name of another member of The Wolves scrawled in — what I assume is — his handwriting. "I'll give you a choice, Princess. Either you behave and come with us, or we can stay and have a little *chat* with George when he gets home. Take your pick."

She's stilled in Everett's grasp, her hazel eyes bouncing from the brass knuckles encasing my brother's dominant hand, to the gun, still clutched in my grasp. She's chewing on her bottom lip, a nervous habit that's making my pulse accelerate as her brown waves dip in front of her face, hiding her from my view. *Am I really fucking doing this?* "I'll go, just don't hurt him, please."

"If you misbehave again, or try to run, this deal is off, and I'll come back for him, got it?" I wait for her small nod of agreement before motioning for Everett to move, my legs stalling as he pulls her out of the front door. Reaching into the bag, I pick out a single chip and drop it on the ground with her discarded pepper spray, a warning, and a silent message for her father. *He fucked with the wrong family.*

A crowd has gathered on the sidewalk, their curiosity getting the better of them, but the quick wave of my gun has them scrambling like roaches back into the holes they crawled out of. I let out a low growl as I climb into the passenger seat of our black SUV, dropping the heavy bag at my feet.

Everett is waiting in the driver's seat, white-knuckling the steering wheel, and the girl is in the back, separated from us by a thick piece of tempered plexiglass.

"What're you going to do with her?" Everett is quieter than normal, his thumbs tapping against the wheel as he waits impatiently for my response. What *am* I going to do with her? None of this was supposed to fucking happen.

"Just drive," I snap, risking a glance over my shoulder. My eyes meet the hazel orbs of the girl cowering in the backseat, and I'm lost in their color for a moment. *Femme fatale.* She turns away, her legs lifting to her chest as Everett begins to maneuver us down the road, but I can't seem to pull my gaze away from her. Her face and arms are nicked with cuts, her knees and hands raw and bloodied. Her jeans, which appear to have already been ripped, are torn open further, the right pant leg now split up to the middle of her thigh. The plain blue tee that she's wearing clings to her curves, and her large bust strains against the fabric so that it's become almost sheer, the outline of her lacy bra visible through its stained cotton. She kicks her leg out, having caught me staring, her foot connecting with the tempered glass.

"She's fucking spirited, that's for sure." I turn back around, shamelessly adjusting the bulge that's tenting my pants, and shake my head as Everett throws a knowing smirk in my direction. *Fucker.*

We hit a pothole, the dilapidated road jostling the car and causing my shoulder to slam against the window beside me. I curse, opening my mouth to chastise Everett on his shitty driving, when I realize that he's trying to adjust himself, too. *Looks like I'm not the only one staring.*

"Eyes on the road, Brass." I allow my eyes to drift past the windshield, taking in the town that flies by outside, watching as her world disappears behind us.

It's an hour's drive back to our home, and the sixty minutes that trickle by seem to drag on for an eternity. Once the car is parked, and the garage door is shut, I get out, pick up the duffle bag off the floor and slam the door shut behind me. Everett pulls the rear door open and moves aside so I can peer in at Brielle, who's still firmly planted in her seat.

"Out." I bark the order, my voice harsher than I intend, but she ignores me, her eyes locked on the headrest in front of her. Everett laughs from behind me, enjoying the power struggle exchanged between the two of us. "Don't make me repeat myself, Princess. Patience isn't something I have an abundance of." She casts a glare in my direction but doesn't move, her arms crossing over her chest. "Fine."

I reach into the car and encircle her waist, pulling her from the backseat and tossing her over my shoulder.

She screams, "Put me down!"

Her small fists pound against my back, but they're easy to ignore as I carry her into the house and move into the foyer.

"Where the hell have you guys been?" Rhys' question rings from upstairs, his footsteps loud on the steps as he descends. He nearly falls when he spots the girl struggling and squirming on my shoulder, his foot missing a step so he has to steady himself with the banister. "Beast, who is that?"

I ignore him and move to make my way toward the back hall, letting out an exaggerated and irritated sigh when I hear him following behind me.

"Leave it alone, Blaze," I grumble. The girl is thrashing against me, and I growl as I tighten my hold around her waist, her flailing movements almost making me drop her to the floor. I readjust, planting my shoulder into her abdomen, and stop in front of the basement, slipping the lock out of place so I can yank the door aside. In one quick movement, I set her on her feet and push her into the room, shutting and locking the door behind her before she has the chance to realize what's going on.

"What the fuck are you doing?" Rhys' hand lands roughly on my shoulder, turning me away from the door as her fists begin to beat against the metal.

"She's staying in there until I figure out what I'm going to do." I brush his hand away, needing space to think. *None of this was supposed to happen.* I move to walk past him, but Everett is quick to step into my path, blocking my escape.

"*We* need to figure out what *we're* going to do." Everett corrects, emphasizing his words. His thick arms band over his chest authoritatively, as if *he's* the one that makes the calls. *That's not his burden to carry.*

"This is my mess to clean up, so you two just need to stay the fuck out of it." My shoulder slams into Everett's as I pass him, the duffle bag still clutched in my grasp.

I end up in my study, where I all but rip the bag open, turning it over and watching as the colorful contents spill across my desk. The small, torn piece of paper that flutters out of it, once again, captures my attention. I unfold it so I can stare at the scribbled handwriting that had sealed Beaumont's fate. *Until that girl got involved…*

When Everett and I rolled out this morning, I had no idea I would end the day with a fucking prisoner in my basement. A body to dispose of? Sure. But a prisoner? Fuck, no.

I shove the chips off my desk and sit in my chair, using my laptop to open the email David had sent me. I skim the information again, re-reading the small section about George's late wife and her untimely death, but still, I find no information about Brielle. Closing out the file, I lean back in the chair, rubbing my jaw as I turn to face the wall-length window behind me. *I need to get this mess straightened out, and fast.* There's no denying that the girl is already working her way beneath my skin, and the longer I wait to deal with her, the longer she has to get beneath my brothers' skin, too. I just have to be careful.

Murmured voices float up from downstairs, and although I can't hear them, I'm sure that they're discussing the fucked-up situation I've gotten us in. *I have to clean up after myself.* Growing up, when that rule was originally taught to me by my mother, it was regarding the toys I'd left on the living room floor. After her death, my father twisted her rule to include the bodies of those he forced me to mangle. *Look at this mess, Beast. Clean it up!* I wince, a phantom pain erupting in my back as the memory springs to life, my teeth grinding together as I force the thought back behind its locked door.

I groan as the banging downstairs grows louder, the noise easily filtering through the floorboards as Brielle switches her assault tactic, using her feet now, instead of her hands. *She shouldn't fucking be here.*

I press my fists into my eyes and shake my head back and forth as resentment and guilt rear their ugly heads. We should've just stayed and killed the old man, but how could I have killed him with her there? I wouldn't have done it. The only option would have been to bring him back here, but of course, she had to ruin that fucking plan, too. I smash my fists into my desk, causing some of the chips to scatter to the floor, as an angry yell erupts from my chest. *Fuck.* What the hell am I going to do now?

* * * *

Lincoln

No amount of money is worth *this*.

I dab at my swollen features, attempting to wipe off the blood still lingering on my face, and wince as my fingers strike an exceedingly tender section of flesh below my left eye. *Fuckers.* I growl and drop the rag into the sink, forgoing the useless task of making myself presentable before I limp out of the bathroom. It's late, and although I'd like to grab the nearest bottle of cheap liquor and chug until this pain decreases, I know that I have to wait. *He should be calling soon.*

Limping through my apartment, I wince as I drop onto the couch, my entire body bruised and sore from yesterday's beating. I'm lucky those bastard brothers didn't kill me and will have to ensure that our brief, but terrifying encounter is our last.

"I need a fucking raise," I growl out, dropping my head back against the couch. Heavy thumps of bass are weaving their way through the floorboards from below, and next door, a kid and their parents are shouting. *Paradise.*

I roll my eyes — well, the one not swollen shut — and reach for the bottle of vodka on the floor. *Fuck it.* I flick off the cap and take a swig, my fingers tapping against my jean-clad thigh. *I don't have all night.*

As if summoned by my subconscious complaining, my phone rings in my pocket, and I let out an exaggerated breath of relief. Pulling the phone free, I accept the call and press the cheap piece of plastic to my ear.

"Well?" the familiar voice rattles across the line, tense and demanding, like always. I sigh and roll my neck, taking my time as something clicks repeatedly, nervously, on the other end of the line. "Lincoln."

"It's done," I confirm, gratified by the smile I can hear pull onto his lips.

"Will you see it through? I'll pay you for the trouble." While it's a question, and I *could* say no, I know I'm not in a position to refuse his request.

"How will I update you?" I want to be done with this, and the mystery man on the other end, but that can't happen until my dealer is paid off.

"I'll leave a burner for you at our normal location. Don't contact me from this number again." The line goes dead.

I lift the vodka back to my split lips and pull another large drink from the bottle, groaning as the alcohol burns down my throat. I gulp down a few more swigs and glance at my phone as it chirps, the alert that money has been transferred into my account. *Fuck.* The number makes my head spin, but still, it's not enough. *This prick is going to get me killed.*

Chapter Five

Brielle

I can't believe I signed myself up for this.

The nagging reminder that I *chose* to go in my father's place hounds me relentlessly as I pound against the heavy door, my fists and feet stinging from the repetitive impact. They're not coming back. *No one is saving me from this.*

I scream out in frustration, turning away from the door and dragging my hands along the walls beside me, fumbling in the dark until I can find a light switch. I flip it on, a small bulb above my head sparking to life and illuminating a stairway in front of me that descends into darkness. My heart flutters as I move to the edge of the first step, peering down at the abyss below as I contemplate exploring my new jail cell. What else do I have to lose?

Reaching out, I gently latch onto the railing and start down the steps, stalling halfway as an appalling assortment of scents bombard my nose, the combination so vile that my throat burns with bile as it bubbles up from my stomach. I swallow, gagged by the heavy scent of bleach that overpowers the air-tight confines of the basement, the chemical so thick in the stairway that my eyes burn, and the taste assaults my tongue. Buried beneath the overwhelming, sterile scent, are the earthy undertones of mold, a tangy bite of rust, and some, unknown, repugnant, burning odor, that fills my lungs as I take another step toward the basement floor. It's as I'm cresting the last four steps that I stall, my hand flying up to cover my nose as another, more terrifying scent, pushes past the others to make an appearance, my body stiffening as I recognize it. *Death.* People have died down here.

I don't know why that realization surprises me. I didn't live a sheltered adult life, and I'm certainly not too naive to realize *who* it was that I signed my life over to today. The Grimm Brothers have a reputation that will surely outlive them someday, their devilishly good looks only aiding them in the legacy that they've created for themselves. Living in our neighborhood and attending the community college in the city made it nearly impossible to ignore the stories about their conquests and the massacre of anyone who dared to step in their way. I know that they're gangsters with a taste for blood, just like I know that if I hadn't stepped in today, they would have killed my father. I guess, a foolish part of me just failed to recognize that, in leaving with them, I'd signed my own death certificate. *I'm in here because I'm next.*

A fat tear trails down my cheek, paving a path for the downpour that starts raining from my eyes, my knees quaking beneath me so violently that I have to sit, still clutching the railing for support. *What's going to happen to Samuel, now?* Did he wander back inside to find me missing? Or did he stay, cowering in the overgrown brush, alone and afraid, until nightfall? What did he tell our father? My mind runs rampant with questions, my head reeling as I dance along the edge of a panic attack. I feel like I can't breathe. *Get a grip, Brielle, this isn't over!* I shove my fists into my eyes to stop the tears, and heave in a gulp of air, attempting to regain control over my ragged breathing. *What am I going to do?* Fight? I gave Beast my word that I wouldn't cause any trouble. Would I be breaking that rule if it wasn't *him* that I caused trouble with?

I pull myself to my feet and carefully descend the rest of the stairs, flipping on another light switch once I reach the basement floor. A low hum fills the room as the lights power on above me, row upon row of tube lighting igniting and washing the room in brightness.

I gasp and nearly fall back against the steps. *This is a fucking torture chamber...* The walls and floors are made of thick cement, every visible inch of them covered in enough blood stains to leave the textured gray concrete discolored. Chains and cuffs hang from the ceiling throughout the room, cabinets with padlocks line the walls, and a metal table with restraints stands in the center of it all. I swallow back the panic attempting to surface, and inch further into the room, digging up as much determination as I can muster. *There has to be something in here that I can use to escape. I have to get back to my family.*

Maneuvering around the larger stains on the floor, I make my way toward the wall of cabinets and tug on the locks sealing the doors shut, praying that one will fall off onto my hands. None of them budge, the old wood groaning in protest as I pull, refusing to open. *Fuck.*

"What'd you say her name was?" The question echoes from the top of the stairs, the voice so unexpected that I gasp. I clamp my hand over my mouth and run forward, flipping off the lights so that the room is once again concealed in darkness. I press my back against the wall and hold my breath as two figures step off the staircase, their frames too small to belong to the man who'd locked me in here. *I'm going to have to fight.*

A hand reaches through the darkness toward me, flipping on the switch so the fluorescent lighting washes away the shadows and reveals my position. I don't think, I just act. I throw my fist forward, colliding with the firm stomach of the man closest to me, a loud grunt leaving him as he doubles over from the impact. I scurry back, a yelp escaping me as the brunet from earlier, Brass, steps around his heaving brother, his eyes alight with a mixture of anger and...amusement?

"Brielle, right?" The blond wheezes, his hand rubbing along the spot where I'd struck him. "You're pretty fucking strong... That was a nice hit."

I retreat further back, my confidence waning as he straightens with a chuckle, a corded arm lifting to push his waves back into place. *What the fuck do I do now?*

"We came to take you out of here."

"What are you talking about?" My voice wavers as I reach another wall, the rough cement digging into the thin material of my shirt. After my late night and the emotionally exhausting day, I'm worried I've misheard him. Does he want to help...? I scan them, waiting for one of them to burst into laughter and lunge, showcasing their true intentions, and killing me for my father's supposed crimes.

"I still don't like this, Blaze. He's going to be pissed," Brass mutters under his breath, his arms crossing over his wide chest. He's the shortest of the three men, with a huskier build, and brown hair that's buzzed close to his skull. He glances up the staircase, his hand running along his five o'clock shadow as if he's as on edge as I feel.

"We've already been over this. Did you bring the blindfold?" Blaze brushes off his brother's concern and tosses me an apologetic smile as he snatches a thick piece of fabric from Brass' hand. "Sorry, Flower. This was the only way I could convince him to help me get you out of this room."

My face heats as fear and a new, mysterious feeling pools deep within my stomach, my lip quivering as he twists the fabric around his tan hands. *What is happening?* "You're not putting that on me."

I hope that I sound stronger than I feel, but my legs wobble as Brass' scrutinizing gaze scans me, his eyebrows lifting as Blaze looks over his shoulder to him for help.

"You'd prefer blood-soaked cement to a bed?" Brass' question is harsh, the frustration and unease evident in his features making me flinch. As appealing as it sounds to get out of this hell hole, the idea of blindly following these two lethal strangers is terrifying. How am I supposed to believe that they aren't trying to lure me to my death? *If they wanted me dead, surely they'd have killed me already?*

My eyes jump between the two of them, trying to pick apart their good cop, bad cop routine, my teeth sinking into my bottom lip to keep it from trembling.

With fear constricting my throat, I shake my head, not trusting my voice to reach them.

"If you want out of here, then we're going to have to do this his way, Flower," Blaze states gently. *What is with these men and their nicknames?* I swallow the scream bubbling in my throat, hating that my knees buckle at their choices in name for me, and still as he closes the small distance between us. He holds up the blindfold as if it's a peace offering, an olive branch in the middle of a war, the movement causing his T-shirt to pull tightly over his toned abdomen. My mouth waters needily at the sight. *Fuck this!*

I turn away from him, crossing my arms over my chest as my nipples pebble beneath my bra, an erotic plague of thoughts storming through my brain. "Just get it over with."

I can hear him shift closer, his breath caressing the shell of my ear as his chest presses into my back, the contact causing a spark of nerves to race up my spine. He works quickly, gently tugging the fabric over my eyes, and tying it into a knot behind my head. It's loose enough that if I were to shake my head, the fabric would slip down my face, but if he notices his mistake, he doesn't fix it, his hands lowering to my shoulders so he can turn me back toward the room.

"Don't worry, I promise we don't bite," he whispers, trying to soothe the fear I'm sure he can feel tensing my shoulders.

"Speak for yourself." Brass' growl is closer than I expect, and the surprise makes me jump in Blaze's grasp, a flush of heat creeping up my neck and spreading across my cheeks.

"Not helping, Brass." Blaze sighs. Blinded, the scents of the basement seem stronger, the hands on my shoulders warmer, as I cling to what senses I have left. He pulls me to a stop just as my sneakers connect with, what I assume to be, the bottom step, his long fingers around my shoulders loosening ever so slightly. "This would be easier if I carried you."

"I can do it," I bite out, yanking my shoulders free of his hold.

Reaching forward, I grasp onto the railing, lift my foot, and attempt to take the first step, my unease making me clumsy. I pitch forward before I've made it up the first step, the toe of my shoe catching on the lip of the stair, gravity knocking me forward before I have the chance to catch my balance. The wood of the stairs is unforgiving as I crash onto it, a low hiss of pain escaping through my teeth as my already sore, scabbed knees throb and break open from the impact.

"Dammit, Blaze, just pick her up!" Brass barks from above me.

A low sigh fills my ears as an arm snakes around my waist, then I'm lifted to my feet, my shoes planted back on the floor as his previous sigh of annoyance melts into a light bout of laughter.

"Would you prefer I throw you over my shoulder, or can I carry you as a woman should be?" Blaze's flirtatious voice is hot against my ear, sending a shiver of desire through my body. I chew on the inside of my cheek and groan, barely resisting the urge to stomp my foot and throw a temper tantrum like a child.

"Do *not* throw me over your shoulder." I'm pouting, my lips flattened into a tight line as I try to ignore the reaction he's pulling from my body.

"Are you sure? It looked like you were having fun earlier," he jokes, slowly replacing his arm around my waist. He lifts me, scooping my legs with his other arm as he cradles me against his chest, his long fingers brushing against the exposed skin at my side.

"Oh, did it?" I question sarcastically, falling for his playful banter, *You should be scared, not cracking jokes.*

"Well, yeah, of course. Isn't hitting and kicking someone the universal sign that you're fucking ecstatic with your current situation?" He adjusts me in his grasp and starts up the stairs, ignoring them as they creak in protest beneath our combined weight.

"Can you two knock it off? Beast will snap our fucking necks if he catches us." Brass snaps. Blaze grumbles something under his breath so quietly that not even I can hear him, but nods, the basement door creaking as it's pushed open.

I'm carried forward, the footsteps of the men echoing in unison as we cross through their home. I can't focus as he carries me, distracted by the comforting, gentle caress of his fingers along my skin, and the spicy smell of his cologne, my stomach twisting as I'm unexpectedly carried up another flight of stairs.

"I've got you," he murmurs, somehow able to sense the unease wrecking my system. His arms tighten around me, pulling me so close to his chest that my cheek brushes against his shirt, the heat of his body warming my already flushed face. *Fuck.* Why is his kindness so comforting?

Soon after we reach the top of the stairs, I'm set on my feet again, the carpet beneath me so plush and lavish that my sneakers sink into it. Freshly washed linen and lavender scent the air, a stark contrast to the horrifying, grimy basement, and my hands work to pull the blindfold away from my eyes. When my eyes have adjusted to the light, I gasp, quickly taking in the new space. *This room is huge.*

Large windows with pink-tinted curtains let in the late afternoon sunlight, the natural lighting warming the space and welcoming me in with gracious arms. A king-sized wooden canopy bed sits in the center of the room, the mattress covered in white and beige blankets and brown leather throw pillows. Green abstract paintings hang on the wall above the bed, tying in the colors of the pillows thrown haphazardly on the fluffy white armchair in the corner of the room, and a neutral rug peeks out from beneath the designated seating area. There are two other closed doors in the room, one to the right, and one to the left of where I stand, but I doubt either would aid in my escape.

"We'll leave you alone to get situated. If you need anything, just shout, okay?" Blaze is standing in the doorway, blocking Brass, who's hovering in the hall with a nervous scowl warping his face. *I get to stay here...?*

"And Beast? What about him?" The fear and excitement that fills me at the thought of disobeying him confuses me.

I watch Brass open his mouth to respond, but Blaze is quick and beats him to it. "Don't worry about him. We'll take care of it."

I want to question him further, but before Brass can make or add a bitter remark, Blaze shuts the bedroom door, sealing me away, once again. I stand there for a while, too dumbfounded to move, my eyes locked on the door as if they may reappear through it at any moment and strike. Of course, they don't, and when my unease has passed, I march forward, a new determination quickening my step. I try to turn the handle, but it doesn't budge, the black knob so untarnished and clean that it looks like it could be new. *Did they do all of this for me?*

Annoyed, I spin away from the door and walk toward the beckoning windows, my heart fluttering as I stare down at the garden three stories below. Even if I were desperate, there'd be no way for me to jump without injuring myself... Should I even bother checking the rest of the room? Surely they wouldn't have gone through the trouble of replacing the lock and door handle if there was another way for me to get out. Right? *I have to be sure.*

It doesn't take long to search the two additional spaces, a walk-in closet and a spacious en suite — complete with a soaker tub and shower — before I collapse onto the mattress, exhausted.

When was the last time I lay on something this *soft*? I let out a small sigh, but despite the enveloping mattress, I can't get comfortable, my mind racing with thoughts of my family. What are Sammy and my father doing right now? Were they able to find each other? Are they safe? *Are they mourning me...?*

I squeeze my eyes shut before the tears can start, and grab a pillow to press over my face in a lame attempt to keep the sobs at bay. I can't keep crying like this is the end. I'll figure something out, I have to. I just...need to sleep first.

I roll onto my side and kick off my shoes, letting them drop to the floor as I struggle to settle. I replace the pillow beneath my head and let my mind slip, the mattress and the sheets molding around the curves of my body soothingly. I push away the worried thoughts that keep me awake, and instead, try to focus on an escape plan. I'll have to win their trust if I want out of this room, but *what* is it going to take to earn it?

Chapter Six

Rhys

"Can you make enough for me? If I'm going to get my ass beat because of you, the least you can do is feed me dinner."

Everett is sitting at the island behind me, his fingers drumming noisily against the kitchen counter as he scowls in the direction of the stairs. He's never been much of a rule breaker, especially where Xander is concerned, and always acts pissy when he's nervous or on edge. He's going to have to grow a pair of balls if he's ever going to convince Beast to give him more responsibilities. I roll my eyes at his request, but grab another pack of hamburgers from the freezer, straightening and dropping the frozen meat onto the counter.

"Burgers? What if she's vegetarian?"

"Do you really think she's a fucking vegetarian, or are you just trying to twist my balls? She stood her ground against Xander — if she doesn't like it, I'm sure she'll say something." I knew, even before Everett filled me in on what happened this afternoon, that Brielle Beaumont was different. If watching her disarm my brother's normally calculated composure wasn't enough to prove it, hearing the way that she sacrificed herself for her family certainly was.

"Maybe a bit of both?" His drumming picks up, a disjointed melody with no end in sight.

"Do you want to cook?" I keep my voice cool despite the irritation I can feel flaring to life in my chest. I love both of my brothers, but I've had just about enough of their shit today. Not only was I intentionally left out of their planned 'meeting' with Brielle's father, but I also seem to be the outlet they've chosen to take their anger out on today, and I'm not sure how much more of it I can take. He doesn't respond as I shut the freezer, so I shrug, and yank open the fridge, rifling through it in search of the cheese, lettuce and tomatoes I know we bought earlier this week.

"You're arguing over what to make her for fucking dinner?" Xander's booming question doesn't startle me. I've known him for too long to be surprised when he suddenly pops into the middle of a conversation, even if it's one I wasn't prepared to have him overhear.

"Yes." I grab the food I'd been searching for and turn from the fridge to find him standing at the edge of the kitchen, fuming. His face is red and his jaw is clenched, his arms crossed over his large chest as he glowers at me and Everett. "Are you finally done pouting in your office?"

"Pouting? I was trying to figure out what the fuck I'm supposed to do with that girl!" He explodes, marching toward me in a fit of rage that I've come to expect. I thrust my shoulders back, refusing to shrink beneath his scrutiny, and eye him as he stops in front of me. He's taller than me, and a whole hell of a lot stronger, but I know the truth hidden behind his anger. I've seen the broken child that he tries so hard to disguise.

"That *girl* is named Brielle, and while we're on the topic, it's probably best if you know that we moved her into a guest suite upstairs —"

"You took her out of the basement?" His attention snaps to Everett, who is quick to hold up his hands in surrender.

"Giving her a room is the least we could do after *you* stole her from her house. She's not our fucking enemy, Xander," I curse, regaining his attention.

"You weren't there this morning. We think her father is affiliated with The Wolves. We found a duffle bag full of our chips stashed in their house. He's been stealing right from underneath our fucking noses!" His gaze is unyielding, watching as I carefully step to the side, putting space between us.

"So, we're condemning people based on their father's mistakes, now? You of all people shouldn't want us to implement a rule like that." The sting of my statement strikes him as if I've delivered a physical blow, the air leaving his lungs in a sharp exhale through his teeth.

"Rhys." Everett's warning slices through the tension in the room like a knife, but I can't bring myself to regret my words, even as Xander takes a defeated step back and his angry demeanor begins to wither.

I know I need to back off. Arguing with him when he's like this won't get us any closer to finding a solution, but I can't stop the words that begin to spill from my lips. "I have never questioned you about anything, Xander, but I am right now. I will *not* help you punish that girl for someone else's mistakes."

"She did this to herself." He's so quick to spit out the defensive remark that I'm sure it's running on repeat through his head, a low growl rumbling from his chest as he stares at me, exhausted. "What would you have done?"

Everett's mouth parts in surprise before he can catch himself, his shock mirroring my own as Xander's words echo through the kitchen. *What would I have done?* Is he asking for help...?

I take in a small breath and let a few silent moments trickle by, needing the time to stifle my anger. *Anger won't get us anywhere.* I have to seize this opportunity while I can.

"We shouldn't be focusing on how the situation could've turned out. What we *should* be doing is figuring out where to go from here, and until we can all come to some sort of agreement on what to do with her, we need to at least attempt to get along with her." My voice is light as I tread carefully into this uncharted territory, feigning confidence while also attempting to ensure I don't cross any invisible boundaries. This is the first time that I've ever heard Xander ask *anyone* for their input, and I don't want to step so far out of line that I ruin Everett's chance at having the same opportunity.

"We'll never agree on what to do with her," Everett grumbles from the island.

"Maybe not today, but this isn't a decision we should be rushing into. Her life deserves more than a five-minute debate." I counter.

Everett has stilled in his chair, his palms pressed flat against the countertop as we wait for Xander's response. Sure, I can toss my suggestions around, but ultimately he is the one who will have the final say. If he wants her dead, she'll be buried six feet under in less than two hours.

"I'll give her one week. That should be more than enough time for me to figure out if she had any part in all of this," Xander finally agrees.

I can't help the sigh of relief that leaves me. His submitting is the only evidence I need to realize that she's already begun picking at the locked door he keeps himself hidden behind. "Why don't you go upstairs and see if she'd like to eat with us, Xander?"

"Me? Why can't you fucking do it?" he snaps, slipping back into the broody alpha male role he was forced into.

"Because you're the one that's going to have to learn to get along with her. Go up there, invite her down, and please, *try* to be civil. I'll get the burgers started." I throw him a cocky grin and turn toward the back door, ignoring the angry curses he tosses in my direction as I go.

I slip outside and seal the warmth of the house in behind me, content, as I stare up at the orange-pained sky overhead. I settle by the grill as I start on dinner, the fire spilling up from the grill, warming my skin. Is Brielle upstairs watching the sun lower over the horizon? Is she looking out, wondering how much time she has left? *At least I bought her one more week.*

I knew the moment that I saw her squirming on Xander's shoulder, fighting and cursing him, that she *might* just be the key we need to unlock him from the chains dragging him down. I'm just going to have to hope that one week is enough time for her to win my brothers over.

"You're wiser than you'd like people to believe." Everett joins me on the back deck, hovering by the door as he watches me quizzically. I ignore him, still a little more than pissed about the shit storm they've been raining on me all day. "You act like a child, but you're good at negotiating. At talking to people."

"So what?" I question, glancing at him over my shoulder. He shrugs, letting his statement settle in the air, knowing that by allowing the conversation to die, I'll be stuck pondering his words. I can't tell if he's trying to passive-aggressively scold me for not participating more during our meetings or if he's attempting to deliver some other message.

"Can I help?" He's quick to change the subject, crossing the deck to come to stand by my side. When we built the house, we had the contractors create an outdoor cooking space in the hopes that it would give us an excuse to have more guests over. Of course, we soon realized that living and running the world that we're a part of doesn't create the opportunity to develop any relationships outside of our small group. Anyone that gets too close is at risk. That's why we keep to ourselves, preferring to use random women to satisfy our needs when necessary, and keeping everyone else out.

"You hate cooking." I raise a brow at him, watching him with curiosity as he grabs the vegetables I'd set out.

"Better than being inside right now. Xander went up to talk to Brielle, and I'm sure it's not going to end well," he admits with a small laugh.

"Why didn't you go with him?" I glance toward her window, wondering if I should run inside to make sure the situation doesn't get out of hand.

"They're never going to learn to get along if we're constantly breathing down their necks. Let them fight. They'll either figure it out, or they won't." He replies, as if he's not concerned by the seven-day time constraint we have looming over our heads. *He can pretend all he wants.* There's no hiding the worry painted in the brown depths of his eyes.

"He broke into her house and threatened her with a gun a few fucking hours ago. Those are your words, not mine, so forgive me for thinking it's too soon for them to be alone together." I take a step backward and gesture to the grill, my eyes still glued to her window. "Pull the burgers off in five if I'm not back, okay?"

He rolls his eyes but nods, taking my place by the grill as I storm back inside. I can understand wanting them to learn to get along on their own, but Xander is a lot to handle when he explodes. I'm sure a defiant young woman like Brielle is bound to set him off. He's used to the world bending to his will, and she's already proving to be a mountain that won't crumble and grovel at his feet.

"I said, you're going to eat with us!" Xander's shout reaches me at the bottom of the steps, a loud pounding punctuating his demand. *Fuck.* I race up the stairs, unsurprised to see his teeth bared as he beats against her door.

"No, I'm not!" Brielle shouts over his tantrum, her voice unwavering and confident. I can almost hear the smile on her lips. He steps back, an angry growl leaving him as he spots me hovering behind him, his hand gesturing wildly to the door that separates them.

"I tried to be fucking polite, but I'm done playing these damn games. If she won't come out to eat, then she's not going to be fed at all." He's sure to speak loud enough for her to hear, glowering as if he can see straight through to the stubborn woman on the other side. *She's the childish one?* I know better than to test my luck with him a second time today, so I stay silent as he curses and storms down the hallway, his bedroom door slamming shut behind him as he disappears into his room. I let out an exasperated sigh and inch forward, straining my ears to hear Brielle.

She's quiet for a moment, attempting to steady her ragged breathing before she clears her throat. "Brass…? Blaze?"

"It's Blaze. Rhys. My name is Rhys." I wince at my awkward response and lean against the locked door, half tempted to open it so I can make sure she's all right.

"Rhys…can you get me a first-aid kit? I have some cuts that are still bleeding." It's not hard to hear the irritation lacing her tone, but I don't fault her for her anger. She's lost everything. *I'd be pretty pissed, too.*

"Um, yeah, just give me a second, okay? I'll be right back." I start down the hall toward our wing, where I think an old first-aid kit is stashed underneath the sink of the spare bath. It only takes a few minutes to find, but by the time I'm headed back toward her room, Everett is waiting for me.

"Burgers are finished. What're you doing with that?" He nods to the kit in my hands.

"It's for Brielle. Can you throw together a few burgers and bring them up? I think it's probably best if everyone eats on their own tonight." I won't dive into Xander's angry outburst, and I certainly don't mention his threat to starve her for refusing to eat in our company.

"I told you, they're just going to have to work it out on their own," he grumbles, turning and starting back down the stairs. "I'll be back."

I silently thank him and unlock the door handle, raising my hand so I can knock against the wood. "I'm back. Is it okay if I come in?"

"It's your house, isn't it?" Her sarcastic response filters from beneath the door, and I smile. *She's staring death in the face, and still manages to crack jokes?* That's my kind of woman.

I push into the room to find her standing awkwardly in front of the bare mattress, her weight shifting back and forth as if it pains her to stand on one foot for too long. I kick the door shut behind me and scan her, my eyes jumping from her bloodied knees and hands to the plump lower lip she's chewing on.

"What'd you do to your ankle?" My question catches her by surprise. It's not hard to decipher where her pain is coming from, the missing skin on her knees is a minuscule injury compared to the swelling and bruising I can see forming around the base of her ankle.

She raises a dark eyebrow and switches her weight off her right leg. "I tripped."

"I can see that. I guess what I'm asking is if I should call for a doctor."

She scrunches up her nose at the suggestion, the sight making me chuckle as she drops onto the bed behind her.

"It's just a sprain. Can I have that please?" She points to the red kit in my hands.

I pass it to her, watching as she opens it and begins to rifle through its contents. "Wasn't there a comforter in here earlier?"

"Yes. It's, uh, in the bathroom." She glances up at me guiltily, nodding toward the open en suite door. "I fell asleep and got blood on it. I put it in the tub to try to keep it from staining."

"Why are you worried about ruining our comforter?" I lower myself to the floor in front of her, entranced by the ease with which she skillfully cleans her wounds.

"Why are you all trying to eat dinner with your prisoner?" she asks. She's stalled, her ankle partially mended with an elastic wrap as her hazel eyes jump to where I'm seated on the floor.

I can see the uncertainty and unease on her face, her body tense as if she's afraid to hear my answer. *She's scared of us.* "Guest."

"What?" She hisses at my correction, her head shaking back and forth in confusion.

"You're not our prisoner. You're our guest."

Chapter Seven

Brielle

Their *guest*?

I'm frozen, unsure of how to respond as he shifts on the floor in front of me, a small grin pulling at the edge of his lips. I know he's trying to help, and am sure that he's just trying to distract me from my overwrought nerves, but I can't help the bitter question that pops from my mouth. "Do you normally lock your guests up in their bedrooms?"

"We don't normally have guests." He's hesitant with his response, as if there's more that he wants to say but isn't sure how to form the words. "I'll talk to Xander tomorrow and see if we can work out a way to get you free rein of the house, but I really can't push him anymore today."

Xander? Is he talking about Beast?

"I promised him that I wouldn't run. Shouldn't that be enough to warrant me at least a little leniency?" I whisper.

He sighs, running his fingers through his blond waves. "I'm sorry, Flower. It's going to take more than a promise to convince Xander to trust you."

I groan, returning my attention to my swollen ankle so that I have an excuse to avoid the guilt I can see blooming in his evergreen depths.

"Are you sure I don't need to call a doctor?" He looks at me skeptically, his uncertainty in my ability to take care of myself tugging at my frayed nerves.

"Yes. I'm a nurse, I can handle a little sprain." I roll my eyes, surprised by the giggle that seeps from my lips as his eyebrows shoot up in surprise. *Why is he looking at me like that?* Is it because of my nursing degree, or because of the small glimpse I've provided into my life?

A knock at the door interrupts him before he can hurtle any additional questions in my direction. "That's Brass. Everett. I had him bring up some food for you."

He smiles and pushes himself up, his long legs quick to carry him to the door. He's lean, with a muscular build that causes a blush to creep onto my cheeks as I scan the toned arms and legs proudly displayed by his clothing. When he pulls open the door, he steps aside so Everett can squeeze into the room, a plate of burgers clutched in his hands. My stomach growls at the sight of the food, cursing me for my missed meals and light breakfast. *I'm starving.*

"I didn't know how hungry you'd be. If you want more, there's still plenty left." Everett's voice is softer than I've heard it, his brown eyes jumping around the room as he tries to look anywhere but at me. I can see the regret on his face but it's going to take a lot more than a few burgers to make me forget the way he stood by and allowed his brother to kidnap me. Rhys, seemingly able to pick up on my unease, takes the plate from his brother and strides toward me, setting it down on the bed beside the first-aid kit. His spicy scent overwhelms the food but disappears as he backs away, his eyes finding Everett by the door.

"We'll get out of your hair so you can eat." Rhys offers me a small smile before turning toward his brother and nodding as they share some form of unspoken communication.

"Wait." The request pops out of my mouth before I can stop it, stalling them both. *What am I doing?* I glance at the burgers beside me and let out a defeated sigh. "Do you guys want to eat with me?"

"I thought we weren't supposed to eat with our prisoner?" Rhys raises a brow and crosses his arms as a playful smirk pulls onto his lips.

"I thought you said I was your guest?" I grab the burgers and lower myself to the floor, setting the plate in front of me and gesturing to the space across from me. "So? Did you expect me to eat four burgers by myself?"

I toss the last bit at Everett, smirking as he chuckles nervously. "I wasn't sure how much you'd eat."

He follows Rhys' lead, sitting on the floor in front of me and taking a burger from the plate.

"Next time, try remembering that I'm not a man." I wave a hand at myself, earning a light laugh from them both as I grab myself food and lean back against the bed.

"We're very aware that you're not a man, Flower." Rhys' voice is low as his heated gaze lingers on my lips, a soft gasp escaping as a twinge of excitement sparks to life deep in my stomach. I squirm under the caress of his longing stare, enjoying the sensation of his eyes burning a hot trail along my lips and down the length of my neck. *What the fuck am I doing?*

Guilt quickly entraps me, ripping me from my trance and slamming the door shut on the want that had begun taking root in my core. Yes, I need to earn their trust, but allowing them to flirt with me, and flirting back, is taking two giant steps in the wrong direction. *I have to keep moving forward.*

"You're not a vegetarian, are you?" Everett asks, breaking the awkward silence that has filled the room. He nods to the burger grasped gingerly in my hands, his brown gaze still avoiding my own.

"No, not a vegetarian. I'm just making sure Rhys doesn't keel over before I dig into mine." I joke. Rhys nearly chokes on the food in his mouth, a muffled laugh making its way around the bite of the burger as he shoots a worried glance at his brother.

"I didn't poison it!" he declares, his eyebrows furrowing as if offended by the suggestion. He takes a giant bite of his burger to prove his point, raising a brow at me and nodding toward mine. "See? Now eat."

Demanding much? I dig in despite the annoying order, almost moaning as an explosion of flavor bursts across my tongue. We did our best in our family to pinch pennies, so that meant we didn't purchase a lot of meat that wasn't already ground up to make it more versatile. I don't think I've had a burger since I purchased one at a fast-food restaurant after a late-night studying session with my fellow nursing classmates.

"Even if you had, I'm sure Flower here knows a few ways to pump a stomach. Did you know she's a nurse?" Rhys seems proud as he pops the last bite of his burger into his mouth.

"A nurse? What made you decide to do that?" Everett's question is one I've dreaded having to answer since the moment I enrolled in my classes. I know that a simple answer would satisfy as a response, but the truth is much more complicated. How do you explain that you *can't* be an idle spectator while someone's life drains out of their eyes, again? *I can't tell them.*

"I've always wanted to be a nurse." I trip over my response, making the lie even more apparent. Growing up, I'd dreamed of becoming a librarian like my mother. I never pictured pursuing a career like the one I've ended up in.

"Sure, just like we've always wanted to be gangsters." Rhys nods, tossing me a look that screams *I can see straight through your bullshit.*

I shrug, brushing off their curious stares as I finish my burger and gesture to the bare bed behind me. "Since I'm your *guest*, I don't suppose there's another blanket you could get me for tonight?"

"What happened to —"

"She's currently drowning hers in the bathtub," Rhys interjects, jabbing a thumb in the direction of the en suite. "You're sure you don't want to use that one? If you change out the water, you could make it into a heated blanket."

"What kind of mobster doesn't know that hot water *sets* a bloodstain?" I'm looking at Everett now, his brown eyes reluctantly lifting to meet mine. They're dark, an earthy color that seems to change as we watch each other, morphing into a lighter, milk chocolate as he smirks.

"I think Mrs. Claebourne put a spare set of blankets in the linen closet. If not, I'm sure Rhys wouldn't mind volunteering to keep you warm for the night." Everett's lighthearted and suggestive joke makes embarrassment weave through my veins. *He can joke?* I didn't think it was possible!

"Mrs. Claebourne?" I question, ignoring the way my heart thrums at the implication hidden in his words. I grab the last burger and bite into it greedily, uncaring if either of them had wanted to claim it for themselves.

Everett tenses, as if he's given away something he shouldn't have, but Rhys waves off his concern by gesturing to the luxurious room we're sitting in. "You didn't think we're the ones that keep this place clean, did you?"

"I guess it *is* pretty spotless," I mumble, returning my attention to the burger in my hand. A maid might just be my ticket out of here.

"Are you still hungry?" Rhys has pulled his knees up to his chest, his muscular arms wrapped around his legs as he watches me finish the last of my food.

I shake my head and wipe my grease-covered fingers off on my ruined jeans, sighing as I realize that my first real paycheck is going to have to be spent on my wardrobe. I guess that's *if* I live to see my freedom again.

A shrill beeping sound pulls me back, the unexpected noise making me jump as Everett fishes a cell phone out of his pocket with a curse.

"Fuck, I'm going to be late." He shuts off the alarm and pushes himself to his feet, his phone quickly re-stashed within his pocket as he gives me an apprehensive once over. "Thanks for letting us eat with you."

I can't suppress the laugh that bubbles to life at his awkwardness. A small nod is all I can manage as he backtracks toward the bedroom door.

"Blaze, don't forget the blanket."

Rhys salutes his brother, only rolling his eyes once he's disappeared through the door and his footsteps have disappeared down the hall.

"Why do you let them order you around?" My voice is soft, my eyes following him as he grabs the empty plate and stands.

"I'm the youngest, so they've been bossing me around for a long time. I guess I just got used to it. Don't worry, Flower, it's nothing I can't handle." He winks, shuffling toward the door.

"For being the youngest, you're certainly the most level-headed," I grumble, thinking back to Beast's frequent outbursts.

He smiles at me sadly, as if he's able to discern the thoughts running through my head. "I'm going to run this downstairs, and see if I can find that spare blanket. Do you need anything while I'm down there?"

"A glass of water would be nice." I delicately push myself up and sit down on the bed behind me, watching as his face contorts.

"Fuck, yes, water." He looks regretful as he realizes that one of my basic needs has been neglected. "Sorry, Flower. I'll be right back."

He mumbles the apology as he slips into the hallway, the door latching shut behind him as another door slams in the distance. I wince, prepared to hear Xander's shouts of anger at catching his brother leaving this room with an empty dinner plate, but nothing happens. No shouting ensues, and no curse words are flung. The hallway is silent.

I let out the rush of air that'd been trapped in my lungs, thankful that, at least for today, the shouting seems to be behind us. Maybe Xander is starting to realize that shouting at people won't make them listen.

I pull my legs up onto the bed and stifle a yawn, exhaustion seeping into my limbs as I stare at the door. Now with food in my stomach, the soft cushion of the bed beneath me seems more alluring and welcoming than it had earlier, the short nap I'd taken only leaving me more tired than I'd been before drifting off. *I want to sleep.* What is taking Rhys so long? Maybe he can't find any blankets. A small giggle bubbles past my lips, Everett's words from earlier echoing through my head as my eyes drop to the new door handle they must've installed, just for me. *Lucky girl.* It's as I'm staring at the sleek, black metal that a thought explodes to the surface, demanding and screaming for my attention. *Rhys didn't lock the door.*

It takes me a millisecond to process the realization, then I'm bursting from the bed, scrambling to my feet as adrenaline surges through my system. I race toward the door, uncaring of my thundering footsteps, and throw my hand toward the unsuspecting handle, gripping it tightly and turning it. It doesn't resist, allowing me to pull the door open.

It's not until I place a foot in the hall, that another thought whispers through my mind, stalling me halfway out of the door. *What if this is a trick?* Slowly, I lift my eyes to scan the hallway, my hand still clutched tightly around the handle. I'm half expecting to see a disappointed Rhys waiting for me, or a fuming Xander, but as I finish scanning the hall, I'm relieved to find that it's empty.

I suck in a silent breath and retreat backward, closing the door with a soft whimper as I mentally battle with myself, knowing I might not have another opportunity like this.

"Fuck," I curse, wiping a stray tear off my cheek as I stomp toward the bathroom, pissed at myself, at them, and the fucking world. I know that one of them is probably waiting, ready to catch me if I try to bolt, but what happens if I keep waiting and die before another chance presents itself?

I slam the bathroom door and sink to the floor in front of the tub, dropping my head into my hands with an angry hiss. *I just want to go home.*

"Brielle?" Rhys' voice sounds from the other side of the door, tentative and unsure. I lift my head, prepared to tell him that I want to be left alone, but he doesn't give me the chance, pushing into the room without any further hesitation. "What's wrong?"

"You can't just barge in on people while they're in the bathroom. What if I were taking a bath, or peeing, or something?" I shake my head at him, wiping my fingers across my face to ensure that no salty trails of betrayal have been left behind.

"I was supposed to believe you were in here taking a bath with the comforter?" he jokes, offering me a sad half-smile as he crouches down in front of me.

I let out a soft breath and purse my lips, turning around to inspect the blanket behind me. "I suppose it's been soaking for long enough. I should probably get it out."

"Let me help you," he offers, leaning over and unplugging the drain.

The water starts gurgling, and he's quick to begin wringing out the blanket, his muscular arms flexing as he works. I'm lost for a moment, just taking him in, before I realize that I'm gawking and get to work helping him. We eventually get the tub drained and the blanket wrung out. He cradles the wet fabric to his chest, carrying it as delicately as he'd carried me as he heads back to the bedroom door.

"It's starting to get late. I'd better let you get to bed, Flower. I'll see you in the morning for breakfast." He smiles, nodding toward the new blanket waiting for me.

"Thanks, Rhys... I guess I'll see you in the morning." I watch him leave, turning away from the door as it shuts behind him, the lock clicking quietly into place. I cross the room and run my hands along the soft, black fabric of the new blanket he'd brought for me, and pick it up, the smell of their laundry detergent floating up. Something falls to the floor, and when I look, I see an oversized T-shirt and a pair of sweats have fallen out of the neatly folded sheet, a water bottle lying on the bed where the blanket had previously been concealing it. *Thanks, Rhys.*

I peel out of my shirt and ruined pants, unfastening my bra and dropping it on top of my other clothes. I slip into the clothes Rhys left for me and chug the entire bottle of water. Wrapping myself in the blanket, I crawl into the center of the bed and surround myself with pillows, my eyes quickly becoming heavy as I drift off into a surprisingly peaceful sleep.

* * * *

Lincoln

Fuck. Fuck, fuck, fuck, fuck, *fuck!*

I curse inwardly, the hands around my camera shaking as I round the house again, hoping, *praying,* that I'm wrong. Of course, with my luck, I'm *not* wrong. George Beaumont is pacing his living room floor, a single, green casino chip clutched in one hand, and a cell phone in the other. He looks miserable and pale, maybe even a little mortified, but he's still breathing. Alive. That means…

The burner phone in my pocket vibrates, and I bite back a groan when I see the single initial that lights up the screen. *D*. The money man with no name, no face, and orders that are turning my world upside-fucking-down.

I swallow hard and answer. "D, listen—"

"Don't," he interrupts, his anger palpable through the phone. I inch back through the yard and cross the street, hovering on the sidewalk across from the Beaumont home as George drops helplessly onto the floor of his living room. "You said he'd be dead. They weren't supposed to take *her*."

"I know—"

"Get. Her. Back." He spits out each word as if they're poison, his anger breaking the sentence into three short commands that make my head spin as the line goes dead.

FUCK!

Chapter Eight

Brielle

Coffee?

The smell of a rich, dark roast pulls me out of my dreamless sleep, the late morning sunlight filtering through the curtains making me jump.

What time is it? How did I manage to sleep so well?

I turn toward the smell that woke me and find a red, steaming mug of coffee sitting in the center of the bedside table, a matching creamer with milk waiting beside it. *Was this Rhys or Everett's doing?* While the thoughtfulness of the gesture is something I want to pin on Rhys, the precision of the cup placement and the matching set points to Everett.

Grateful for the espresso, either way, I scoot to the edge of the bed and grab the mug, lifting it to my lips and savoring its flavor. It's delicious, the hot liquid warming me as I push off the comforter wrapped around my legs and stand. The sweats Rhys left for me are large and sag around my hips as I move, my hands tugging at the drawstring absentmindedly while I search for the clothes I'd discarded last night. I walk around the edge of the bed and bend down, prepared to grab the pile of clothes I'd left there last night, but they've disappeared, not a single trace of the fabric left behind. *What the fuck?* I straighten and scan the room, wondering if I'd been so exhausted last night that I'd placed them somewhere else, but it only takes me a second to realize that my shoes are missing, too. *These fucking men!*

"Why would you take my clothes?" I groan, irritated and excited by the idea of one of them wandering around the room while I was asleep. I take a slow sip of the coffee and move toward the bathroom, wanting to wash the sleep out of my eyes, and spot the new clothes folded and waiting for me on the bathroom vanity. "Seriously?"

I set the coffee down and pick up the long-sleeved, olive-colored shirt that's been laid out for me, annoyed that the damn thing is softer than anything I've ever owned before. My annoyance only grows as I realize that it's in my size, as is the pair of black skinny jeans that sit neatly beneath it, but that's not what catches my attention. My eyes bulge. *You've got to be kidding me.* A black bralette with a matching pair of underwear almost blends in with the dark denim, the lacy, skimpy material the only thing differentiating the two items. *I'm going to kill them.* My eyes jump from the shirt clutched in my hand to the saggy, oversized men's clothing that I'm currently wearing. *Goddammit.*

I have half a mind to march to the bedroom door and demand my clothes back, but another, smaller part of me is begging me to get dressed. I've never owned anything like this before and have certainly never worn anything like it in front of three men. The darker, unexplored piece of me wants to get dressed and is begging to make an appearance. *Do I let her out?*

I set the shirt down and glance at the shower behind me, where two fluffy towels are hanging, and bottles of shampoo, conditioner and body wash and a razor are waiting on the recessed shelf in the shower. Yesterday this room had been empty. Did eating with them earn me this? Or were they just *that* unprepared for my arrival?

I don't give myself much time to ponder the questions springing to life in my head. I undress, turn on the water and climb into the shower, letting the warm water caress my body with a grateful sigh. I take my time washing up, carefully scrubbing around my wounds, shaving, and using the shampoo to rinse the dirt and sweat from my hair.

Once I'm finished, I wrap one large towel around my body and use the other to dry my hair, the mirror in front of me covered in a thick fog. I get dressed, unsurprised to discover that the bra and underwear fit me perfectly, too. The olive color of the shirt suits my pale skin, light hair, and freckle-covered face, the fabric stopping just above my belly button, with a neckline that dips low enough to show off the strappy bralette. My abundant cleavage is accentuated by the outfit, and I feel sexy despite myself. I scrunch my waves, attempting to give them shape before I grab my coffee and head back into the bedroom, where I spot a pair of black combat boots sitting in front of the door.

"Is there anything else you'd like me to wear?" I call, feigning irritation as if there *isn't* a smile pulling up the corners of my lips. I grab the shoes and carefully slip them on, glancing up as a light knock sounds on the door. I know better than to be caught off guard when it starts to open, but I can't help the shock that undoubtedly registers across my features when I see that it's an older woman and not one of the guys.

"Well, aren't you beautiful!" She smiles, her hands clasping to her chest as she takes me in at a distance. She doesn't seem surprised by my presence, and I frown.

"You must be Mrs. Claebourne." I take an awkward step back, scanning her, as she had me. She's a plump woman with graying curls lobbed into a short bob around her face, her tan skin wrinkled around her lips and eyes.

"Oh please, you sound just like the boys, just call me Claire. Are you hungry? It's almost time for lunch, but I made some muffins fresh this morning if you need something to tide you over." She offers, walking toward the unmade bed.

"No, I'm okay, thank you." I watch her gather the blanket I'd slept with last night in her arms before she bustles past me toward the door.

"I've got your comforter and clothes all washed for you, although Rhys is pretty sure the jeans aren't salvageable. He said you fell?" She opens the door and starts into the hallway, only pausing when she realizes that I'm not following her. "Are you coming, dear?"

"I—I don't think I'm supposed to leave the room." I feel awkward, my eyes dropping to the floor as I stand on the other side of the open door, wondering, again, if I'm being tested.

"Come on, Princess." Xander's voice makes me jump, my head snapping up to see that he's appeared in the hallway, his black curls falling around his muscular shoulders. He's wearing a pair of jeans and a black dress shirt, the buttons left undone at the top to reveal a patch of chest hair and tattoos that only tempt my gaze to travel lower.

I want to slam the door in his face, but the tone of his voice makes me hesitate. "Don't you want me to stay in here?"

"Are you going to make me regret letting you out?" he questions, his bearded chin dropping so that he can meet my gaze.

"No." I shake my head, my words from yesterday echoing through my head. My promise to behave.

He nods toward Mrs. Claebourne, who's still standing, watching our uncomfortable exchange with a smile on her wrinkled lips. When she realizes that he's turned his attention back to her, she winks at me and turns to head down the stairs so quickly that I almost have to run to keep up with her. I can hear the bedroom door shut, then Xander is following behind us, his footsteps louder than Mrs. Claebourne and mine combined. Rhys, who must've overheard our conversation, is waiting at the bottom of the steps, his blond waves pulled back into a bun on the crown of his head, showcasing his buzzed undercut.

"Morning, Flower!" he calls up to me.

"Did you do this?" I gesture to the outfit as I descend the steps, the smile on his lips and the hungry look in his eyes the only answer I need. "Fucker."

"You don't like it? It's better than my old baggy clothes, don't you think?" He smiles, easily blocking the punch I throw in his direction once I'm close enough.

"I like it," Xander states as he passes, nonchalantly.

I throw an angry curse in his direction.

"How'd you sleep last night, Flower?" Rhys asks. He's waiting, watching patiently as I pause to stare longingly at the door, the forbidden taste of freedom blossoming on my tongue. "We have an alarm system. If you open the door without disarming it, you'll set it off."

"You guys couldn't make it easy, could you?" I hiss, eyeing his hand as he gently wraps it around mine.

"It's not all for you, trust me. We have enemies we have to keep out." He shrugs, releasing my hand once he's pulled me into the living room. He jumps over the back of the couch and lands with a sigh on the soft leather, his feet kicking up onto the coffee table in front of him as he stretches out.

"Enemies? You mean kidnapping people isn't how you're supposed to make friends?" My sarcastic question earns a low growl from Xander, who's hovering, otherwise silently, in the kitchen.

"They come with the territory, unfortunately," Rhys murmurs, patting the couch beside him. I chew on my bottom lip, trying to hide my awe at their home as I walk around the couch and sit beside him, my hand still warm from where his fingers had brushed mine. "Do they fit?"

I tear my gaze away from the room to look at him, his blond brows furrowed together. "What?"

"The shoes. I noticed the ones you were wearing were too small, but I wasn't sure how big to size up." He points to the boots on my feet.

I glance down, only now realizing that my toes aren't crumpled and pinched in the toe of the boot like they would be if I were wearing my sneakers. *How can anyone be that observant?*

"Yes, they do." I offer him a meek smile, overwhelmed by the mixture of emotions that weigh down on my chest. I'm grateful for the kindness and thoughtfulness that he's shown me, but I can't help but be embarrassed, too. It's humiliating knowing that he was able to discern, just from *looking* at me, that my shoes were too small. *What else can they pick apart when they watch me?* My eyes drift to Xander, who's standing by the island, sipping on his own cup of coffee, his mysterious blue gaze locked on me. Is he judging me because of the house and the neighborhood he'd plucked me from? They live in such luxury...what must they think of me?

"Brielle, dear, do you want me to throw these out?" Mrs. Claebourne has reappeared, a laundry basket at her hip, and my tattered jeans in her hands.

"No, no!" I take in a small breath to calm the panic that's risen in my voice, and try to ignore the obvious stares as Mrs. Claebourne replaces them in her basket. "I—I think I can patch them. I'd like to keep them please."

"Of course. I'll get them put away in your room." Her smile is sweet, and she's quick on her feet, disappearing once again out of the room. I hope I can move with that amount of grace when I'm her age. *If I live that long.*

"I don't think a patch job is going to—"

"They're the only pair of jeans that I own, Rhys. I have to try and make them last until I can afford to buy a replacement." I cut him off with a hissed whisper, leaning forward to set my coffee down on a coaster, my gaze dropping to the hardwood floor.

He's silent beside me, making me shift nervously as I contemplate excusing myself back upstairs. I'm about to cave, to race back to the safety of that spare room, when his index finger hooks underneath my chin, and he turns my eyes to him. "Do *not* be ashamed of where you came from, Brielle. Not around us. Not ever."

His tone is so serious that it makes the hairs on my arms stand, my breath catching behind a lump in my throat as his eyes scan my lips. He holds me there for a minute, analyzing me, before he releases me with a sigh and leans away from me.

I frown, my face warm with that familiar rush of heat as I attempt to ignore the twinge of disappointment that fills me when he settles back against the sofa. *I shouldn't want him to kiss me.* So why am I disappointed that he didn't?

"Does Beast know you let her out?" Everett's tired voice sounds from behind us. I whirl to face him, watching as he walks into the living room, his brown hair a tangled mess on his head. "I'm not taking the fall for you again."

He must have just rolled out of bed, the five o'clock shadow sprouting along his jaw and the black sweats on his legs helping corroborate my theory. He turns the corner toward the kitchen, heading toward the fresh pot of coffee, and finally spots Xander, who's still watching me from the island.

"*I* let her out," Xander states, slowly turning his gaze toward Everett as his brow quirks, as if challenging his concern.

"Oh. Well, it's nice to see that you two can inhabit the same space without fighting." Everett moves around his brother so he can pour himself a cup of coffee, his body tense as if he's worried his remark will earn him a blow to the gut. *Maybe it will.* Xander's eyes turn angry as he watches Everett, looking almost as if he could snap him in half for drawing attention to the obvious tension between the two of us. Can he blame

Everett for commenting? This *is* the longest we've been around each other without getting into an argument. I half expect Xander to curse at me for breathing, just to prove Everett wrong, but he doesn't shout or lash out.

Instead, he sets his empty cup down and nods his head in my direction. "Can one of you keep an eye on her? I have a meeting with David to go over a few discrepancies I noticed in the last file I received from him."

"I don't need a babysitter," I interject, but he ignores me as easily as if I'd never spoken.

"I've got her," Rhys pipes up from beside me, his arm tossing over my shoulders so he can pull me into his side. I furrow my brows, irritated as he laughs, distracting me long enough that Xander is able to slip from the room before our new record can be tarnished. *Who is David? What files?*

I have a million questions that I know will never be answered. I turn my eyes back up to Rhys and find a guilty look on his face, as if he can somehow hear my questions, but knows better than to answer them.

He pulls away from me, his fingers running through my hair so faintly I'm not sure it's actually happening as he stands, a smile sliding back into place on his lips. "How about a tour?"

Chapter Nine

Xander

"Open up, David." I don't bother keeping my voice low as I pound on the old man's door, too pissed to care if my brashness disturbs one of his neighbors.

Three of my hired men stand behind me, their heads on a swivel as their eyes scan the empty hall, waiting for their next order. They're not as quick as my brothers, or as intuitive, but their muscles and extensive backgrounds, be it criminal or military, make it safer than marching into uncharted territory alone. Especially if a rival gang is conspiring some kind of uprising.

A lock clicks then the door is pulled open just enough for David's wrinkled face to peer out, a thick chain above his head the only thing keeping me from pushing inside.

"Beast?" His eyes grow wide with realization, and he quickly shuts the door, making an annoyed huff race through my teeth. *Guess we're doing this the hard way.* I lift my foot, prepared to kick down the door, when the sound of the chain sliding out of place echoes through the silent hall, and the door is pulled open again. "Come in."

He waves us into his home, eyeing my goons nervously as they pass him before he shuts the door behind us. "What're you doing here?"

"George Beaumont, the man I asked you to get information on. Something was missing from his file, and I want to know why." I scan the small apartment, my nose wrinkling with disgust at the smell of cigarettes that assaults my nose. *This place is fucking filthy.* Empty cans and food trays litter every available surface and cigarette butts cover the floor. I *know* he makes enough money to afford a nicer place than this, or at least a fucking maid, so what the hell is he doing with his paychecks?

"Missing? I sent you everything —"

"Did you?" I interrupt. The color leaches from his face at my accusation, and despite the dimly lit room, I can see the way his eyes bulge and whirl toward the computer sitting behind me.

He swallows, his throat constricting as he nods certainly. "I did."

"Then would you care to explain why the report failed to mention that George has a child? Where are the files, David? How long have you been withholding information from me?" I bark stilling David in his place as he attempts to process what I'm throwing at him, his chest frozen as if he's too scared to breathe. *Good.* He should be scared.

"I — I wouldn't betray you like that, Beast. My loyalty has always been to you and yours." He stumbles over his feet as he hurries forward, falling into the old chair in front of his desk, clumsily bringing his computer to life. "I always send you anything that I think is pertinent."

"So you thought that his daughter wasn't important enough to mention?" I manage to keep my voice even, which seems to rattle the old man more. A thick bead of sweat begins to collect above his brow as he pulls up different screens.

He points to the computer, where he's managed to load a small report on Brielle, and an even smaller one on a boy — her brother Samuel. "I thought his kids were dead."

His answer drops a weight into the air that I can't explain, my stomach twisting as a million new questions spark to life. Kids? *Dead?*

"I can assure you that Brielle Beaumont is very much alive. Why are these reports so short?" I question, watching as his fingers type wildly against his keyboard.

"There hasn't been any recent activity under either of the Beaumont children's social security numbers for six years," he mumbles, his eyebrows furrowing in confusion.

I'm standing over him, close enough to tell that he hasn't showered in a few days, and try my best to follow the mouse as he scrolls through other screens. "What does that mean? My brother said the girl is a nurse, so she must have gotten a degree from somewhere recently. There has to be information on that."

"I'm sorry, Beast. If these two kids are alive, someone's been deleting any documentation tied to them, or they've been locking it away in a server that *I* can't even see." He scratches his neck, his eyes glued to the report so he has an excuse to avoid my gaze.

"Why would someone do that?" I know that I'm reaching, trying to pull answers from a man that doesn't have them, but none of this makes sense.

"Why does anyone hide or delete anything?" he asks rhetorically, shrugging as he finally glances up at me. "Whoever is doing it, doesn't want anyone to know that they exist."

The sudden realization that *someone* wanted to keep Brielle hidden from me makes that familiar heat rise in my chest. "Is there a way to track where it's going?"

I'm grasping the back of his chair, my head reeling. *Who* and *why* would someone try to hide her? A sick thought pops into the back of my mind, but I refuse to acknowledge it. *I wouldn't fall for it.* I can't place the blame on her, not yet. Not until I have more information. And yet...even as I tell myself to ignore the signs, it's impossible to forget the circumstances that led to Brielle ending up in my home. The stolen chips, the incorrect documentation, her father being *out* when she leaped through that back door... *Was it all a setup?*

"Let me see what I can do. It'll take me a few days, maybe even a week if I run into the firewalls I'm expecting to find." David stretches in his chair, oblivious to the war waging in my head. Did I bring a snake into my home to wind a deceptive trap around me and my family? A snake disguised as an innocent daughter who's been waiting for the perfect moment to strike?

I blink, watching as the old man begins typing again, ignoring us as we let ourselves out of his home. I can't wait to see what information David *might* find. I need answers, and I need them now.

I have to clean up my mess.

* * * *

I don't remember the drive home. I don't remember ordering the three men with me to restrain my brothers. I don't remember pinning Brielle against the living room wall or pressing my loaded piece against the side of her skull. All I *can* remember is red.

"Who do you work for?" I growl the question, clicking off the safety without relieving the pressure of the heavy metal from her temple. I have her wrists pinned above her head with one of my hands, her heaving chest pressed against mine as I stare down at her hateful, hazel gaze.

"I don't work for anyone," she grits out. She's not struggling like I expected her to be, and she's not begging for her life either. If she's aware that I've caught on to her little game, she's doing a damn good job at keeping herself composed.

"This is insane, Xander! Let her go so we can talk about this," Rhys shouts from behind me. Two men are struggling to hold him back, his blond waves spilling out of his previously tidy bun. He's fighting to get free, his green eyes dark with a mixture of hate and anger. This is hurting him. *I'm* hurting him.

I swallow the guilt threatening to suffocate me and do my best to ignore Rhys as he shouts at my back. Brielle winces, the first sign of fear flashing through her eyes. "I will do anything to protect my family, Princess. Do you understand? I suggest you start fucking talking."

"I guess that's something we have in common," she whispers, tilting her chin up so that she can meet my burning gaze. She sucks in her bottom lip, burying the fear that had threatened to boil over only a moment ago, and leans into the gun. "Do what you have to do to protect them."

I gape at her before I can catch myself, my jaw clenching as her response renders me speechless. *Why does she always have to keep me on my fucking toes?* I have a gun pressed against her head, and she's not fucking breaking.

"Xander, please." It's Everett who speaks up this time, his voice a quiet surrender. He's not struggling like Rhys, but I can see a storm brewing in his brown gaze. I finally look at my brothers, *really* look at them, my teeth grinding together as a twinge of pain jolts through my chest. I have to keep going. I *need* answers.

"My hacker thought you were dead." I swallow, turning my attention back to Brielle. "Someone has been hiding information on you for *six* years, and I want to know why."

I hope that the little explanation will ease the pain I had seen warping my brother's features, but Rhys is unrelenting behind me.

"You promised us one week," he shouts, pulling at the guilt he can somehow spot buried deep within my chest. I growl, attempting to keep my composure, but the hand clutching the gun begins to shake as my father's voice shouts through my ear. *Clean it up, Beast!* I have to protect them, even if this hurts them.

"M-my mother died six years ago. I don't know if that has anything to do with the missing information, but it's the only thing I have to offer you, except for my word, that I'm *not* who you think I am. I'm not here to hurt you, or your family," Brielle whispers, her eyes watering as she glances up toward my weapon. She trembles in my grasp, goosebumps rising across her exposed flesh as if a cold breeze just swept across her, the mere mention of her dead mother enough to cause her confidence to waver.

"If you put a bullet in her skull, Beast, you'll be turning your back on us. Do you really want to turn out like your father? You gave us your word." Rhys' words strike me to the core, dousing out the relentless flames of my anger as if the wildfire within me were nothing more than a candlestick. The red starts to diminish.

I look at the girl in my grasp and let out a rough sigh, realizing with a finality that I *can't* hurt her without hurting them. Dropping my gun from her head, I release her, the movement so sudden that she's unprepared. She crumples at my feet, her hair falling in front of her eyes as I tower menacingly over her. "The only reason that I'm letting you walk away is because I made a promise to my brothers. I won't go back on my word."

She winces at my voice, her fingers rubbing the sting of my grip from her wrists, but nods her understanding. I turn away from her pathetic display, and wave at my hired muscle, signaling them to release my brothers. Rhys' gaze burns me as he brushes past me to kneel beside Brielle, his fingers delicately tracing over her arms.

"Get her to her room, and meet me in my study. We need to talk." I don't wait to hear Rhys' snide response or the murmured apologies he throws into Brielle's lap as he gently tugs her to her feet. I jab a thumb in the direction of the door, and start up the stairs, knowing my men will get the hint and leave. *I'm done with them for today.*

Everett is hot on my heels as I turn the corner and head down the hallway, not giving me enough space to breathe, let alone think, as we finally make it to my study. He posts himself in front of the door, his arms crossed over his chest as he watches me. I pour myself a double shot of whiskey from the bar in the back of the room, down it, and refill my glass, allowing the burn that tracks down my throat to distract me from the pain wringing my chest. I'm not ready to believe a word that Brielle said, but I can't keep torturing my brothers like this, not when she's so obviously worked her way under their skin. *I can't kill her.* Not in front of them. *How the fuck am I going to fix this?*

I almost don't expect Rhys to join us. Ten minutes pass before he stalks into the room, slamming the door behind him so aggressively that I expect him to lunge at me, or at the very least get in my face. Instead, he takes Everett's place in front of the door and nods in the direction of the empty glass clutched in my hand.

"Pour me one," he orders with an authoritative growl, his shoulders pressing back as he stands taller under my gaze. I don't have it in me to argue with him, or to demand that he remember who's in charge. I simply grab the decanter, pour a second glass, and pass it to Everett so he can hand it to Rhys. "You'd better start explaining what the fuck is going on."

I haven't taken orders from anyone since my father died, and a large part of me is pissed that he suddenly thinks that he can boss *me* around, but I'm not going to push him any further away than I already have. Gritting my teeth, I allow his outburst, and pour myself another shot, reminding myself that they're the only family that I have left. I go over what little information David provided me with, but despite the explanation, I can still see anger flickering in their gazes.

"There's no way that Brielle is a spy for The Wolves." Rhys' disbelief is evident as he shifts on his feet, likely wanting to pace, but too afraid to move out of the way of the door. After what I just pulled, I can't say that I blame him.

"Look at the evidence in front of you, Blaze. Don't let your cock cloud your fucking judgment. She's only been here for one day and she already has you wrapped around her fucking finger." I can't keep the venom out of my voice as I take another pull from my glass, my temper threatening to boil back over.

"*You* need to look at the evidence. Did you see the clothes she came here in? The shoes? Nothing fit her, everything was old and too small. She wouldn't be worried about saving those ruined jeans if she could afford to buy new ones. You know as well as I do that if she were one of their moles, she'd be getting huge fucking paychecks," he objects, tossing back his shot of liquor.

"Maybe spying for them wasn't her choice. What if her father had to prove himself to them as a part of his initiation? *She* wouldn't be reaping the profits if this is all part of her father's hazing. She'd just be a pawn in their bigger game." Everett's voice is low as he hesitantly suggests that Brielle is more of a coerced accomplice than the conniving enemy I believe her to be, his gaze avoiding my own as he pours Rhys another drink.

"Have we checked the Beaumonts' bank accounts? Is there any money moving within them to solidify these accusations?" Rhys questions.

I let out an irritated sigh. "There aren't any accounts in Brielle's name that David can find. As for George, the only recent deposits have either been from his job or what little he earns from gambling. The man spends a lot of time in our fucking casinos." I can see the spark that lights up Rhys' gaze, and know, without asking, that he believes the lack of monetary transactions is enough to prove their innocence. I, however, will not be persuaded so easily. "It's not difficult to open an account under a false name if you have the right documentation. Or he could be getting paid in cash."

"Do you hear yourself? Why is it so fucking hard for you to believe that not *everyone* is out—"

"I will not make my father's mistakes! I will *not* be stabbed in the back by someone I let into my own fucking home." I shout, cutting off his words. The alcohol is doing nothing to tamp down the anger boiling through my veins, the anger engraved in my fucking *genes*.

"She is not one of them," Rhys states with a finality that makes me believe he's ready to drop the conversation. I glance up at Everett, hoping to see that he at least understands where I'm coming from, but he's not looking at me. He's watching the floor as his mind wanders, no doubt attempting to come up with a solution to the predicament *I* put us in.

"You can't be so sure," I hiss.

The space falls silent as Rhys and I stare each other down, still hot with anger as Everett paces absentmindedly, lost in thought. I'm desperate to march into Brielle's room to demand more answers, but I remain planted in place, knowing that doing so will only drive the wedge growing between my brothers and I in further.

"Something else is going on here…" Everett mutters. We all stand there, attempting to piece together the puzzle that's fallen into our laps, each of us on a different page, and all of us tiptoeing around each other in fear that this could break us apart.

Rhys finally meets my gaze again, his normally lighthearted personality doused by the anger clouding his features. "You have to fix this. We have to figure this out, and soon."

I can almost hear my father's voice spilling from his lips. *Look at this mess you made, Beast. Clean it up!*

Chapter Ten

Brielle

I start searching for a way to escape the moment Rhys locks the door behind him. *I can't risk staying here one more second.* I make quick work of re-scouring the room, searching for something, *anything*, that can be used to help me escape, but of course, like yesterday, I find *nothing*. It seems that, despite providing toiletries and a first-aid kit, the Grimm Brothers were still careful enough to ensure that I'd still have nothing that could be used to pick the lock.

"Dammit!" The curse is warped by fear and anger, a garbled cry leaving my chest as I wring my hands through my tangled hair. *What am I going to do?* He's going to kill me.

I can't help the tears that sting my eyes at the thought, and it's all I can do to keep them from falling. *It won't help.* Right now, I need to focus. My life is hanging precariously in the balance, and I'm not sure that Rhys' soft spot for me is going to be enough to convince them to let me survive another night. I *have* to escape.

I pause in the midst of pacing the floor, a line tracked through the carpet behind me, and glance toward the light pouring in from the bedroom window as I realize what I have to do. *I have to jump.* My gut writhes, the coffee in my stomach churning, but as I inch toward the window and glance out at the ground three stories below, it's the haunting E.R. stories I was told back in school that make the world sway beneath my feet. A fall from this height *will* break my legs and, if I land wrong, I could even fracture my spine. I have to do something to cushion my landing or find some way to shorten the fall if I'm going to make it off of their property unscathed. *Stop overthinking. Just do it, Brielle, now.*

I swallow around the lump in my throat, forcing away the burning nausea attempting to suffocate me, and search for a way to open the windows. When I find the locks hidden on either side of the frame, I click them open and slide the pane up with a satisfying *clunk,* gasping at the unencumbered view of my drop. Cool autumn air swarms me, bringing with it the calming scent of leaves and rain, as I flatten my shaking palms against the windowsill. It's as I'm poking my head out of the window that a petrifying thought freezes me in place, panic surging through my veins anew. *The alarm system.* Do they know I opened a window?

I glance over my shoulder, tense, but when I don't hear any thundering footsteps or shouting, I assume that I somehow didn't manage to trip a silent alarm. *They didn't expect anyone to be going in or out of the third-story windows.* I release the air that had been trapped in my lungs and steel myself as I take one final look around the room.

I scan the blanket on the nearby chair and the made bed and an idea sparks to life like a fire finally catching to ignite. *If I want to shorten the fall...*I grab the freshly washed comforter and yank, pulling it off the bed with one swift movement. Dropping it to the floor at my feet, I move around the room and quickly collect the other blankets. With a plan in mind, I tie the pieces of fabric together, using them to create a makeshift rope that I secure to the metal bed frame. Once it's secure, I toss the opposite end out of the window, and step back to inspect my work. A shorter fall, but not by much.

A light knock on the door makes me freeze with one knee on the windowsill, my heart leaping into my throat as I stare at the wooden door. *What the fuck do I do?* "Leave me alone."

My voice is hesitant, despite being nearly certain that it's Rhys on the other side. When he brought me back up here, he showered me with enough apologies to drown me. I demanded space, needing a moment to talk myself off the ledge I was walking. Nothing he said would fix what had happened, and I couldn't stand listening to him apologize for his brother's actions.

"It's just me," Claire calls through the door. *I'd forgotten she was here.* Did she seen what happened? I quickly push the blankets toward the corner of the window, hoping that the flowing curtains will obscure my obvious attempt at escape. She doesn't wait for me to respond and pushes into the room with a serving tray clutched in her wrinkled hands. It's not hard for her eyes to find the makeshift contraption strung from the bed to the window behind me, but instead of rushing from the room to find one of the brothers, she holds up the tray. "You should drink something before you go."

Her smile doesn't falter as she crosses the room and sets the tray down on the bare mattress, her small hands lifting a purple tea kettle in surrender.

"I've always believed that tea soothes the soul," she explains, pouring the tea into two small mugs.

There's not a cup of tea on this planet big enough to soothe my soul... I offer her a meek grin as she passes me a steaming cup, the smell of honey floating up with the steam.

"You're very brave, dear. I heard what you did for your family, for your father..." She trails off as she settles herself on the edge of the mattress, her eyes once again scanning the mess of blankets behind me.

She doesn't seem at all surprised to have caught me attempting to escape, and although she hasn't called one of the guys in here to turn me in, I doubt she'll be willing to let me go, either.

"I'm not," I finally murmur, taking a small sip from my cup. It's a warm chamomile tea, a flavor I recognize from my childhood that instantly relaxes the tension headache building within my skull.

"Call it what you like, but I've never seen anyone willing to stand their ground against Xander." She shrugs, her tireless smile faltering.

"What happened to him to make him so untrusting and cruel?" I can't stop the question. I *know* that people aren't born hateful...so what broke him and turned him against the world? *Who* broke him?

I can see the hesitation in her eyes, the questioning glance toward the door as she contemplates telling me something I may or may not deserve to know. She scrunches her nose and shakes her head solemnly.

"He says a lot of things in anger, dear. You'll have to decide for yourself whether or not you'll listen to the Beast his father created." I don't have much time to ponder her response or ask her any clarifying questions. She stands, her gray curls bouncing around her face as she walks toward the bedroom door. "You need something to eat. I'll bring up some lunch for you."

"Oh, but I'm not—" My response is cut short by the door closing behind her. "Hungry."

I let out a huff of air and set my cup down on the tray, uneasily glancing back at the open window. *The Beast his father created?* She may have been vague, but I understand what Claire was tiptoeing around. His *father* broke him...

I shake the thought away, refusing to acknowledge the sympathy and compassion that try to overwhelm me at the realization. "Having a shitty father doesn't excuse his actions."

I have to escape before it's too late. I grip the rope of blankets and lift one knee back up onto the windowsill, my eyes once again scanning the drop as I try to prepare myself for what I have to do. Of course, it's nearly impossible to ignore the small voice, that tiny part of me locked deep in the recesses of my brain, that tells me to stay. *To fix it.*

A low string of curses flows from my mouth as I drop my foot, once again, to the bedroom floor, easily pulling the bunched fabric back into the house. With an annoyed grunt, I slam the window shut, making the glass vibrate within its frame. *What is wrong with me?* The question I've asked myself a thousand times since arriving here floats through my head again, this time in bright, red, angry letters. It's a question I don't have the answer to, and I'm too confused to try to figure it out. *These brothers are making me question everything.*

I cross through the bedroom toward the en suite, my makeshift rope lying in a noticeable jumble on the carpeted floor. I know I should, but I can't bring myself to care about the possible consequences I could face if one of the brothers finds out about my attempted escape. *What'll they do, kill me?* The thought forces a crude laugh from me as I draw myself a bath, peeling out of the new and unfamiliar clothing while hot water fills the porcelain tub.

It's a free-standing soaker tub and takes a few minutes to fill, but as soon as it's ready, I slip in. It's almost too hot to enjoy, my skin instantly pinkening as the water rises to cover my chest, nearly reaching the tip of my chin. I breathe through the heat, letting it swallow me as I cling to the bite of pain that allows a momentary distraction from my racing thoughts. *What is wrong with me?* That damnable question won't leave me alone. I take a small breath and slide down the tub until I've dipped beneath the water's surface. *What is wrong with me?*

Chapter Eleven

Everett

She tried to escape.

I can see the evidence balled up on the floor by her bare bed, a rope of blankets tied together that she must have dangled from the unlocked window. Our conversation had been so heated, so distracting, that we hadn't heard her open it. She *could* have escaped…so why didn't she?

I'm hovering on the opposite side of the bathroom door, where I can hear water sloshing in the tub she must be soaking in, unaware—or uncaring—that someone is in the room with her. *She stayed.*

I turn back toward the room, lean against the door, and scan the discarded sheets, my eyes rolling involuntarily as an annoyed sigh escapes me. She could've at least *tried* to hide her intentions. If Xander had been the one to see this, whatever small amount of control he has left would snap. There's no questioning how he would perceive her actions—he'd assume his earlier accusations were correct and accuse her of staying to mole out more information on us. He'd kill her first and ask questions later. Rhys, on the other hand, would see this and impulsively decide to let her go, too guilt-ridden to think of the possible consequences releasing her could cause. I find myself stuck somewhere in the middle. I'm not ready to believe that she's an enemy we need to fear, but I'm also not ready to let her out of my sight, yet. Keep your friends close and your enemies closer, right? I just have to decide which side of the fence she falls on.

"Everett?" Mrs. Claebourne sounds surprised to see me, her eyes jumping between where I stand and the balled-up blankets on the floor.

I can see the beginnings of more words forming on her lips, no doubt a lie to cover for this mess, but I press a finger to my mouth, ordering her to keep quiet. If Brielle hasn't realized I'm here, I don't want to startle her, especially after her altercation with Xander.

I wave my hand toward the blankets as I cross the room to where she stands in the doorway, and growl, "Can you get that cleaned up before one of my brothers find it, please?"

I don't attempt to hide my irritation with the situation but, despite my obvious frustration, the woman seems to relax at my words. She lifts a wrinkled hand from the plate of food she's holding to squeeze my arm, a small thank you slipping from her lips as she walks past me into the room.

I wait for a moment, watching as she scurries across the carpeted floor to set the plate of food down beside the abandoned tea before getting to work untangling the sheets. It's not lost on me that she must have realized Brielle's intentions, if not for the way that she reacted when she saw me, then simply because the fresh tray of tea proves she was here after Rhys joined us in the study. *I'll have to remember her soft spot for our prisoners in the future.* But...is Brielle really our prisoner? Sure, she's locked away in this room right now, but she's being fed and clothed and has a bed to lie in. Our prisoners *never* receive those luxuries, and they certainly never make it out of that basement alive.

I squeeze the bridge of my nose and stifle a groan as I step into the hallway, spotting Rhys, who's finally emerging from the study down the hall. I'd left a few minutes after the conversation ended, unable to stand the uncomfortable silence or the hateful glares my younger brothers were exchanging. *This is all new for us.* I can't think of a time when we've been divided like this, not over our businesses, not over our respective backgrounds, and certainly not over some *girl*.

"You surprised me back there." Rhys sounds exhausted, his lips drawn down in a frown as he stares at his topped-off glass of whiskey. "You've always been quick to take Xander's side, but you finally voiced your own opinion. I'm not saying that I agree with what you said, but..."

He shrugs, his freed blond waves falling around his face as he shakes his head. As much as it pains me to admit, he's not wrong. Most of the time our family dynamic works because we're loyal to each other to a fault. When Xander saved my life all those years ago, he not only earned a brother, but a man willing to follow him to the darkest pits of hell and back. That's why, when he makes a decision, even if it's one I don't full-heartedly agree with, I back him up. It's the least I can do after what he's done for me. This decision involving Brielle is the first thing I've ever *openly* disagreed with him on, and the only reason that I'm doing it now is because I can't get her out of my fucking head. *I'd like to bend her over my knee for trying to escape.*

"I think she's in the bath." I'm not ready to face my truth—that I'm a broken dog willing to piss and shit wherever my master orders, so I brush off his statement in favor of buying Mrs. Claebourne more time. The only question is, out of everything I *could* have said, why did I say *that?* I'm sure the budding erection sprouting in my jeans at the thought of her bent over for me has *nothing* to do with it.

"Do you think she's okay?" His question makes my stomach lurch as his eyes move to the door behind me, his eyebrows knit together.

It doesn't matter how much time has passed, Rhys will always be the child seeking to provide the comfort he was deprived of.

"She's in the *bath.* Do you want me to go in there and ask her?" My voice is heavy with sarcasm.

"Not unless you have an invitation, otherwise, I'd have to kick your ass." The ghost of a smile lights up his green eyes at his chivalrous words, and the sight is enough to ease the tension building within my chest.

"You'd fight me regardless. Don't act like *me* receiving that invitation wouldn't piss you off." I smirk, leaning into the playful banter as Rhys' angry demeanor begins to melt.

"We've never been opposed to sharing before." He shrugs, laughter spilling from us both into the otherwise silent hallway.

At the sound, Mrs. Claebourne appears in the doorway behind me, giving me an inconspicuous nod that lets me know the coast is clear. The old woman, always so intuitive and knowing, must have realized I was stalling. She clears her throat and weaves her way around us, our uncontrolled cackling only resuming once she's rounded the corner out of sight.

After we've caught our breath, Rhys lets out a long sigh and runs his fingers through his messy hair. "I should grab her some fresh clothes to relax in."

"Why don't you go in there and check on her? I'm sure I can find something," I reply, understanding his need to comfort while also knowing that she's more likely to accept his kindness than mine. I, after all, had a hand in uprooting her from her family and the only life she's ever known.

He doesn't waste any time. As soon as I've stepped out of the way of the door, he disappears into the room, shutting the door behind him with a quiet click that leaves me alone, once again. I run a hand across my stubble and sigh, heading down the hall toward my room.

It's the last door on the left, a minimalist space that I've decorated with such a sparse amount of wooden furniture that the room feels almost unwelcoming. Aside from a king-sized bed that takes up residence in the center of the room, the only other pieces of furniture I've allowed myself to purchase are a matching nightstand and a single chest of drawers. It's impossible, despite the wealth my brothers and I share, to stray away from the frugal lifestyle that's been ingrained into my core. I watched my parents struggle my entire childhood to keep food on the table and a roof over my head because of their spending addictions. I will *not* allow myself to become homeless or go hungry again.

I reach into the chest of drawers, pushing back the flashbacks that threaten to surface, and grab one of the few graphic tees that I own, and my only pair of joggers. The nearly empty drawers slide open and closed easily, allowing me to grab a pair of socks before I head back down the hall.

When I enter Brielle's room, I'm not surprised to see Rhys sitting on the floor in front of the bathroom, his legs crossed in front of him as he taps on the wood in front of him.

"I'm not leaving until I know that you're okay, Flower. Don't make me come in there." Rhys calls, glancing up at me as I stop beside him. "The door is locked, and she won't talk to me."

"I'm sure that she just wants to be left alone, Blaze." I try to keep my voice gentle, but the urge to scold him is balancing precariously on the tip of my tongue. *She needs space.* Who wouldn't after what's happened? Pissing her off is only going to make things worse. I'm about to open my mouth and tell him that when the bathroom door is yanked open, and an annoyed Brielle appears in the threshold, a white towel wrapped firmly around her body.

"I'm fine. See?" She tosses her wet waves over her shoulder, the droplets slipping down her bare arms to the fluffy material hiding the rest of her from view. Her face, although puffy from crying, remains unaffected as she stands, practically naked in front of us, her annoyance overpowering any awkwardness she might feel.

I swallow hard. The towel is doing nothing to conceal her curvy figure, her flawless skin only marred by the bruises beginning to darken her wrists and temple.

"What is that?" The question is directed at Rhys, who's still sitting on the floor in front of her, too dumbstruck to move. He's unable to mask his reaction to her, his mouth hanging open as his face flushes with color.

It takes him a few seconds to recover, but eventually he rockets to his feet and holds out the forgotten glass of alcohol still clutched in his hand. "Whiskey."

She takes it from him, the movement causing the towel to fall slightly down her body as she lifts the glass to her full, pink lips. I watch in amazement as she takes a small sip, savoring the taste for a moment before she tosses the rest of the drink back, her face impassive as the burning alcohol slides down her throat. Now it's my turn to gape at her.

"Are those for me?" Her hazel eyes are on me, assessing the pile of clothes in my grasp as she hands the empty glass back to Rhys.

"Yes." I fumble over my words as my fingers brush hers, the warmth of her skin against mine making my cock jump in my jeans, an unwelcome surge of desire curling through my body.

She's hesitant at first, her hands running along the fabric as if she's waiting for us to say something, but when we don't, she adjusts her towel and disappears back into the bathroom. The room grows cold once the door shuts behind her, and Rhys glances up at me with a smile, a low whistle ripping from his lips as he winks up at me.

"I heard that," Brielle shouts through the door as if her scolding is supposed to embarrass him.

When she re-emerges, dressed in my clothes, I can't help the twinge of excitement that ripples through me anew. I *like* seeing her in my clothes, but I'd prefer to see her in *nothing*.

"I'm—"

"If you apologize one more time, Rhys, I might have to rip out my fucking hair." Brielle cuts off his words before they're even out of his mouth, her socked feet padding against the carpet as she crosses the room.

I can see the tentative way her eyes scan the made bed and her fingers shake as she lifts the sandwich left for her by Mrs. Claebourne. When her gaze returns to the unlocked window, I can *feel* the deep-seated want within their depths to my core.

"I had Mrs. Claebourne re-make your bed for you. When I came in, I realized the blankets looked a little *out of place*." While I *want* her to know that her escape plan didn't go unnoticed, I *don't* want her to feel the fear I can see creasing her forehead. Her whole body is tense, her eyes widening as she watches me, waiting for the moment I reveal her intentions and ruin whatever trust system she's built with Rhys. "You'll learn I'm a bit of a control freak. I hope you don't mind."

"I haven't noticed," she replies sarcastically, trying to conceal the relief I can see flooding her features with little success. If Rhys notices, he doesn't comment, choosing instead to lean against her bed frame as she takes a small bite of her sandwich.

"You will," I murmur, watching in amusement as her face flushes. She sways on her feet, chewing another bite as Rhys laughs beside her, jumping into a conversation to ease her nerves.

I walk toward her unlocked window, partially listening to what they're saying, and look down toward the backyard, a large knot forming in my gut. The length she'd been willing to go to escape... *She's scared of us.*

I glance back toward them and notice her watching me from the corner of her eye, her hand shoving at Rhys as he says something to embarrass her. I laugh, although I didn't hear what was said, and start to turn away when something catches my eye on the ground below. I look down, searching for the fallen leaf or bird that had caught my attention, but see nothing. *It must have been the wind.* I shake off the feeling creeping up my spine and lock the window, turning back to them as Rhys pokes Brielle in the side. It's at the joyous sound of her giggles that my decision is made for me. *She's innocent until proven guilty.*

Chapter Twelve

Brielle

Laughing hurts.

I can feel my chest tighten as Rhys cracks another joke, oblivious to my stomach knotting as too many overwhelming emotions threaten to suffocate me. Physically, I'm fine. A little bruised, yes, but it's mentally that I'm falling apart. I *shouldn't* be so at ease with these men. I shouldn't be *drawn* to these men...but it's impossible to ignore the temptation, and connection, that builds within me every second I'm with them. I should have escaped when I had the chance.

"Are you okay, Flower?" Rhys' laughter has died off, his concerned gaze scanning my face.

He's sitting on the floor beside me, our backs against the bed while Everett sits across from us, observing our interactions with a meek smile. *What am I supposed to say?*

It would be easier to shrug off his concern, jump back into the conversation I've fallen out of, and pretend like nothing's happened, but lying to them is only going to break me. I have to open up if I want to prove that I'm not here to threaten and betray them. If I'm going to earn their trust, I'm going to have to give mine in return. "Honestly? No. You guys make me question *everything*."

They both seem caught off guard by my response, their eyes locking in that bonded way that shows they're having a silent conversation before Rhys clears his throat.

"You make us question everything, too." The shot of whiskey I taken from him doesn't dampen my surprised reaction to his words. My face flushes and my chin drops as he scoots closer to me. "It's nice to know the feeling is mutual."

"What do I do about Xander?" The question slips past my lips but, even as it floats in the air, I'm unsure of the true intentions behind it. Am I asking them how to navigate his obvious hate toward me? Or am I asking them how I could begin to have him start questioning things, too?

"You give him time." Everett's simple response manages to answer all the questions I didn't realize I was asking. *I give him time.*

I look between the two brothers, the weight on my shoulders relenting a little with his statement. I can breathe easier, and almost hear the silent promise hidden in his words. *I* have time. Whatever stance Everett had on my situation seems to have wavered in my favor.

Two down, one to go.

"We won't let him touch you again." Rhys' voice is steely, his hands balling into fists in his lap. His jaw is tense, and all traces of his humorous demeanor have vanished.

I grab his hand without thinking, comforting him when I know that I should be running in the opposite direction. I shouldn't be *relishing* in how natural this feels, how warm his skin is against mine. This should scare me.

Two sets of widened eyes scan me as I chew on my bottom lip, my face warm with the heat beginning to pool between my legs as a suggestive joke drips from my tongue. "What if I want him to?"

I try to tell myself that my words are nothing more than what I intended them to be, *a joke*, but I realize as I sit there, nervously awaiting a response, that I'd be lying. To my surprise, Rhys laughs, his angry facade shattering.

"As long as you're into it, Flower, that's all I care about." He shrugs, his thumb stroking the top of my hand.

All right, maybe the alcohol *is* working. Up until this point, I'd been shoving away any vulgar thought that sparked to life when I re-imagined Xander pinning me against the wall. I should've been terrified, and *only* terrified in that situation, but there's no denying the way my stomach lurched when he pressed against me. The way my breath caught in my throat when he trapped my wrists above my head, and I was left completely at his mercy.

"It's all new," I murmur, the whiskey making me brave. "How am I supposed to know what I'm into?"

Everett groans, his head tipping back as he attempts to collect himself. "You're not making this arrangement easy, Brielle."

"Good. Neither are you two." I smirk.

"You're an adult. How do you *not* know?" Rhys' voice is thick, an obvious bulge beginning to strain against his pants as he clears his throat beside me.

I drop my head against the soft mattress behind me, unsure of whether or not to jump off the ledge we're all dancing along. Yes, we're flirting, but am I ready to delve into my past with them? *Someone has to break first.* "I've spent the entirety of my adulthood sleeping on a couch, raising my brother, and going to school. I've never had the privacy or the freedom to figure it out."

"You slept on the couch?" Everett questions, obviously remembering the cramped, muggy room he'd stood in.

I tense, momentarily regretting my decision to tell them about my life, but Rhys' unfaltering smile and the gentle squeeze of his hand is enough to ease the ebbing fear.

"What about you two? Did you grow up here?" I swallow hard, pushing away my embarrassment as I change gears, switching the focus to them. I know I need to tread carefully — prying too much could make them suspicious of me, but I *need* to know more about the men who are beginning to break me.

"No." Rhys shakes his head. "We moved here a few years ago after Xander gained control of his father's territory, but we've known each other since grade school."

"Are...you three not brothers?" I stare at them, confused. This isn't the first time that I've heard them mention *Xander's* father, but it's the first I've been able to process their words.

"Nope, just friends who've taken the same last name." Rhys chuckles, tugging me close so he can whisper into my ear, "We could make that foursome you've fantasized about a reality if you'd like."

My face burns as I shove him away. I don't know why I didn't catch on sooner. They don't share any physical similarities, as siblings would, and appear to be around the same age. The only thing they do share is the Grimm last name...and, if I'm lucky, *me*.

I push that thought away before it has the chance to take flight, refusing to delve *that* far into my darker wants, even if it makes my stomach flip. Instead, I elbow Rhys in the side as I settle back against the bed.

"I'm calling bullshit here, Brielle. You can't give us a *glimpse* into your background, just to slam the door shut in our faces. If we're going to give, you're going to give. Deal?" Everett's eyebrow tips up as the curve of a smile pulls onto his lips.

I know I might regret this, but what do I have to lose? "Okay, deal. What do you want to know?"

"Why don't we go back to the conversation you tried to steer us away from? You didn't have a bedroom back at your house?" Everett's question makes me flinch.

"Um, no. When we moved, it made more sense for Samuel to have the second bedroom, so I took the couch. From what my father's always said, he didn't plan on us being there for long, but...debt doesn't disappear overnight." I look down at the long, tan fingers still encircling mine, and trail upwards until I'm scanning Rhys' trimmed beard and high cheekbones. "My turn?" I wait, watching as Rhys nods encouragingly before I ask, "Who does Xander think I am?"

"An informant for The Wolves," Everett replies so smoothly that I almost think he's joking. If it weren't for Rhys tensing beside me, I'd have started laughing.

I don't have to ask them who The Wolves are—just like I learned of the Grimm Brothers, I learned of the numerous other gangs that run rampant throughout our city. *Why does he think I'm some kind of mole?*

"My turn," Rhys pipes up, eager to change the subject. "What did you want to do with your life, Flower?"

I remember the awkward response I'd given when Everett had asked why I'd become a nurse, the secondhand embarrassment making me sigh as I drop my eyes back to our hands. "I wanted to be a librarian."

I expect them to laugh, but they don't.

"Then…why did you get a nursing degree?" Rhys whispers, but I shake my head, unwilling to give them that answer.

"Why didn't you let Xander kill me?" I ask instead, deflecting his question.

I know that I'll have to tell them the truth if I'm going to continue opening up to them, but I can't help prolonging the inevitable. I don't want their sympathy, and I certainly don't want their pity. They're the first people who've seen me for the woman that I've become despite my past, and I'm not ready for that to change.

They take so long to respond that I don't think I'm going to get an answer, the room growing silent, making me worry that I've pushed them too far. I'm ready to tell them to forget it and move on to another line of questioning, but finally, Everett sighs.

"We've been trying to change the way that Xander sees the world for a long time, Brielle. It seems that, in two days, you've managed to get under his skin in a way that we never could. Even if we *hadn't* stepped in, I don't think he would have killed you. You're changing him, you're changing all of us." Everett's admittance makes my heart ache.

I'm changing them? They're changing *me*.

"All right, Flower, no more stalling. Why did you become a nurse?" Rhys is unrelenting, rephrasing his question as he tugs on my hand so that I'll look up at him.

"I—"

I'm interrupted by the bedroom door opening as a pissed-off Xander appears in the doorway. His long dark curls are pulled back into a bun at the nape of his neck, and his black dress shirt has been replaced by a plain long-sleeved tee that somehow manages to show off *more* of his muscular build. "Someone came over the wall on the east side of the property."

His words are enough to send Rhys and Everett scrambling to their feet, their faces set with determination as they start after him.

"Wait! What's going on?" I call, latching onto Rhys' arm before he can make it out of the room.

"Stay here, Flower," he says coolly, his lips drawn into a frown as he tugs his arm free of my grasp. I don't have time to argue with him or demand any answers. They all leave, and the lock slips into place behind them as they rush off without another word.

I'm overwhelmed with questions, my forehead pressing into the door as I try to ignore the words that float through my head with warning. *We have enemies we have to keep out.* Rhys made it clear that their world was dangerous…is this one of the many rivals he'd mentioned needing to keep out?

I want to help them, want to prove my innocence… but how?

* * * *

Lincoln

She's alive.

I pause to catch my breath, a strenuous task when my already out-of-shape physique is paired with injuries, and lean against the tree towering over me. My body is screaming with exhaustion and my head pounds with the desire for more alcohol, but I can't touch another drop until this is done. *I have to get this over with.*

I pull my camera out and turn it on, loading the image display on the back so my most recent photo fills the small screen. Rose looks unchanged from the last time I photographed her, and I'm hoping that confirmation of her well-being will be enough to quell D, for now. I pull the burner out of my pocket, snap a picture of the image with the shoddy camera, and forward it to the only number saved in the contact list.

I don't wait long. An order and a death sentence balled into one unpleasant decree flit across the screen as I watch the text come through.

Do whatever it takes. I'll pay what's necessary for my Rose's safe return.

Chapter Thirteen

Rhys

We follow Xander down the stairs in silence, our bodies tense as we mentally prepare ourselves for the battle we believe is coming. Xander is ready, his face set with determination as he clutches his loaded gun, his eyes scanning each window and doorway before he leads us forward. Everett is stiff beside me, his jaw clenched so tightly that I can see his muscle twitching, his dark brows drawn low over his dark eyes. He's attempting to calculate the outcome, needing to overcompensate for Xander's lack of planning and brashness. Me, I'm lost. Focusing is getting me nowhere, and every step I take away from Brielle is only making my thoughts rush back to her, a distraction that could cost me my life.

"Whoever this is, is probably here for *her*," Xander mutters, his words sending a cold chill down my spine. *Here for Brielle?*

"Who would come for her? We took her from the only family member she has that could've tried." Everett's voice is laced with the guilt he'll never admit to feeling, his head shaking slightly as we stop in front of the basement door.

Xander pulls it open, his gun raised as his eyes continue to monitor the hall behind us. "If I'm right about her, it could be The Wolves attempting to kill her for being discovered, or to try to rescue her themselves—"

I interrupt him with an angry growl. My entire body is tense, anger threatening to strangle me as Xander's eyes meet mine, their hardened, cobalt color almost softening in understanding. It's in that quick moment, that I manage to see through his resolve, a small crack forming in his icy exterior before he has the chance to freeze over again. *No one is going to touch her.*

He nods toward the darkened stairwell, the small opening I'd been granted slamming shut as his lips press into a firm line, sealing himself off. "Go."

His order pushes me forward, my feet thundering on the steps as Everett follows close on my heel. After being divided as we've been, I finally feel that—for the time being—we're all on the same page. It doesn't matter who's right or who's wrong...the only thing that matters at this moment is that we protect Brielle.

Once we're all planted on the basement floor, Xander turns and flicks open the switch plate for the solitary light switch, revealing a hidden button underneath. With the press of his thumb, the button lights up, and a loud groan sounds through the room as the bottom half of the stairs begin to lift. *This will never stop being fucking cool.* A small room—a bulletproof armory we had built into the home—

quickly reveals itself. Xander has to curl his shoulders to fit through the doorway, but once he's inside, he grabs the closest loaded weapons and passes them up to Everett and me.

"How many are we dealing with?" I question, counting the bullets within my magazine. I test the weight of the weapon, familiarizing myself with its heaviness before I shove the clip back into place.

"The alarm was only tripped once. Unless a team of them were able to move perfectly synchronized with one another, only one man came over the wall." Xander's voice is tight as he steps out of the room, his eyes rolling over us as he lowers the steps back into place. "That doesn't mean others won't be waiting. I want your eyes open. We stay close and low. Got it?"

"Got it," Everett and I agree in unison.

I roll my shoulders, following Xander as he starts up the steps, my grip tight around my weapon. *Will there be an army waiting? What will happen to Brielle if we die…?* My stomach churns at the thought, leaving a sour taste on the back of my tongue as Xander leads us toward the back door. He slides it open and steps outside first, allowing the cooling autumn air to snake into the house behind us. There's a storm brewing, the clouds cresting and settling along the horizon, threatening to inch closer. *I fucking hate the rain.*

"If this gets ugly, you need to get back here and get Brielle out. She's a caged bird in that room," Everett mutters as he passes me, his gun raised in his steady hands.

"I know," I mumble.

Thunder claps in the distance, and a sigh rushes past my lips as I roll my neck and lift my gun.

Let's get this over with.

* * * *

Nothing.

After an hour of scouring our property in the freezing rain, we find nothing. No armed men are waiting to ambush us, and not a trace of a lingering threat has been left behind. When we get back into the house, we're soaked to the bone, and Xander is beyond fucking pissed.

"Maybe the wind knocked a sensor loose. I'll check the feed," Everett calls after Xander, but he's already storming off, a low growl his only response.

He slams the door shut behind him, a trail of mud and water in his wake. *Mrs. Claebourne is going to kill him.*

I puff out an annoyed sigh, pass my gun to Everett, and jab a thumb in the direction of the ceiling. "I'm going to go check on Brielle."

"You should change first. You look like a drowned rat," Everett jokes as he wrings out his shirt and kicks off his shoes, water dripping off us both onto the hardwood floor. *Correction, Mrs. Claebourne is going to kill us all.*

I roll my eyes at his suggestion and slip off my own sneakers, padding through our silent home while attempting to work some heat back into my body. My fingers and toes are stiff, and my blond waves cling to my neck and face, but the need to see Brielle trumps any desire I have for dry clothes.

My numb fingers fumble with the lock at first, but eventually, I'm able to pull the door open, my frozen body unprepared for the fist that collides with my stomach.

"Rhys!" Brielle gasps, her delicate figure darting back a step as she murmurs a small apology. "I—I didn't... You scared me."

I gulp in a breath, a small smile curling my lips as her face flushes with embarrassment. "Don't apologize. You've got some wicked power in that tiny body of yours."

"What happened? How could you run out of here like that without telling me what was going on?" She chews on her bottom lip, her arms crossing over her chest as anger and annoyance flash across her features. She's pissed, I know, but there's something else hidden beneath her irritated exterior. A fear, for our safety, and *us*.

Whether she's ready to admit it or not, she cares about me, about my *family*, and that realization alone is enough to drive me forward. I close the small distance she's put between us and ignore her angry scowl as I lift a frozen hand to her warm face. She flinches at first, either from the cold, or surprise, but tilts her chin up to me as I band an arm around her waist and drag her closer. She's watching me, and I can see the uncertainty and desire in her dilated eyes as my hand slips around her neck to cradle the back of her head. She's breathing hard, her erratic pants fanning across my cheeks, and I can't fight the intoxicatingly sweet smell of her drawing me in closer. When our lips finally meet, she tenses, and I wait, allowing her inner war to wage before she relaxes into my hold, and leans in.

Her soft hands move to my chest, her fingers sliding along the wet fabric as she presses closer, a soft, breathy moan escaping her lips. I can feel my restraint waver at the sound, a sudden *need* to hear more of those noises hardening my cock. I grab her lower lip between my teeth, tugging on her until I'm rewarded with another soft gasp, her arms wrapping around my neck as my fingers tangle through her hair.

Heat pools through my veins, and I trace her lips with my tongue, a guttural moan rippling from my throat as she pushes herself against the bulge beginning to tent the front of my pants, her lips parting to allow me further access. I deepen the kiss, my tongue tangling with hers, devouring her, tasting her. *Fuck.* I need to slow down.

"Flower," I breathe.

I pull back, enough that I can scan her, and her flushed face. Her chest is heaving, her eyes hooded as they meet mine, and I smile, despite myself. I can't let her earlier admittance slip out of my mind, can't dare to forget her innocence. I'm ready to dive in, but I can't and won't rush her.

"Kiss me." Her voice is a hoarse demand as she watches me through her thick lashes, her heated eyes making me groan.

"I'm trying to control myself, Flower, but you're not making it easy," I mumble.

"So stop trying."

I break with her words, my resistance snapping as I wrap my hands around her legs and lift, hooking her thighs tightly around my waist. I turn, pressing her into the wall as our tongues mesh together in a heated tangle of lips and teeth. Her hips roll, taunting me, shredding my self-control with each delicious thrust of her body against mine. *I want more.*

I drag a hand up her thigh and hover around the edge of her shirt, silently waiting for permission. She gasps at the feeling of my hand, her teeth sinking into my bottom lip with a nod that grants me the access I'd been craving. I slip beneath the fabric, my cold fingers making her shiver as I trail my hand up her body, between the gully of her breasts. I dip my hand into her bralette, her soft whimper hardening my length as I pinch her nipple between my fingers.

She squirms, her needy squeal hardly contained by our sealed lips as she pulls back with a small gasp.

"Rhys." Her eyes are pleading, her teeth digging into her lip as she attempts to form her needs into words.

I can see her urgency growing, and know that the feeling coiling within her is new and unexplored. Her innocence triggers something primal deep within me, and I suddenly have the urge to show her just how fantastic sinning can be.

"I'll take care of you, Flower," I whisper, a promise with more than one intent or meaning. I'm going to take care of her in *every* way that she requires.

Chapter Fourteen

Brielle

This feeling is addicting.

Adrenaline courses through me, pooling in my stomach and heating my core with an overpowering need that I can't understand or explain. My legs and arms feel unsteady around Rhys, and my breathing is erratic as he stares down at me with those heated green eyes. *I'll take care of you, Flower.* His words make my stomach curl with delicious anticipation, blurring any rational thought that could convince me to stop. There's a dark need within me growing with each pass of his tongue along mine. I need *more.*

Rhys' hand slips out from beneath my shirt, and I can't help the small disapproving whimper that falls from my lips with it. He hooks his hand back under my thigh and turns, supporting my weight as he pulls me away from the wall. *Wait, I don't want to stop!* I cling to his neck, but his grip doesn't waver as he carries me across the room, his touch loosening as he lays me onto the bed. *Oh.*

My heart leaps into my throat as he hovers over me, a torn expression contorting his features. "I want you to experience the things that you crave, Flower, but I don't want to overwhelm you. We'll teach you to run, but you've got to learn to walk first."

"W-Where do we start?" I'm panting, his words enticing me as they echo through my head. He'd said *we'll...*not *I'll*, and that realization is doing things to me that I don't understand.

He laughs, my question seeming to ease the worry that had held him back, a smile lighting up his face.

"I have a few ideas." He lowers himself, crawling down my body until his elbows rest on either side of my waist. He winks and pushes my shirt up to press a single kiss to my stomach, before hooking his fingers into my sweats. "I told you I'd take care of you, Flower. I'm going to give you the relief you need."

A flood of excitement rushes through me as he pulls at my pants, my hips lifting so he can tear the fabric down my legs. A groan lashes from his throat as his feverish eyes rake over the black lace covering me, his hungry gaze flicking up to meet mine.

"Are you this wet for me?"

I bite my lip at his words, and drop my head back onto the mattress, my eyes and thighs squeezing shut with embarrassment. He clicks his tongue in disapproval, his hands sliding along the tops of my legs as his fingers reach to skim the soaked underwear I'm trying to conceal.

"Don't hide from me, Brielle."

"Is it...too much?" I whisper, lifting my head just enough that I can peek at him.

He scowls at the question, his hands gently pushing them apart.

"Is your arousal, your reaction to *my* touch, too much?" He growls the question, his eyes never leaving mine as he settles himself on the bed. "No, Flower. Never."

There's a loud ripping sound as his fingers tear the lace away from my body, his green orbs piercing me as he tosses the ruined fabric over his shoulder. I groan, my breath catching in my throat as his gaze finally drops between my legs, a low curse leaving him as he leans into me. Without warning, he flicks his tongue out, stroking my clit for a fleeting second, making my hips buck. He pauses, a smirk pulling onto his lips as he allows me a single, solitary moment to collect myself, before dragging his tongue up my center, tasting and savoring me with a greedy groan. *Fuck.*

He lets out a long breath, his warm exhale sending a pleasurable shiver up my spine as he swipes me again, circling my clit before his lips close over me. I can't contain the stream of moans that pour out of me, his tongue swirling and throwing me headfirst into a world I've yet to explore. A warmth is beginning to spread through me, a new sensation that seems to grow with each expert lap of his tantalizing tongue.

"You're so fucking sweet, Flower," he moans, his words making me flush as I'm carried to new heights. My back arches off the bed, and I roll my hips against him, desperate for more friction. I wrap my hand through his hair, lifting his mouth back to my swollen bundle of nerves, a distressed whimper rumbling from my chest.

"Please, don't stop," I cry out.

He groans, a possessive sound that makes me gasp, as his hands slip beneath my ass to lift me closer to his lips. I'm shivering, my legs quaking around him as I shout, the heat in my belly exploding. Waves of pleasure crash over me, stealing my breath from my lungs, and I cling hopelessly to his hair, anchoring him to me as I ride him through my first orgasm. He doesn't stop, his tongue continuing to swirl around me until I relax in his hold. My limbs are numb, useless piles of jelly, as he crawls across me with a grin.

"Beautiful, Flower. Absolutely perfect." His lips are glistening with my release, and he wipes away the remnants of my orgasm with the pad of his thumb before sucking the digit into his mouth to clean it. My body clenches at the sight.

He chuckles at my expression and drops onto the bed beside me, his fingers pushing back the damp hair clinging to his forehead. *I didn't even realize.*

"Rhys, you're going to get sick." My voice is heavy with exhaustion, but my concern is evident as I pull at his wet shirt. "You need to get out of these clothes."

"Is that an invitation?" He chuckles, his arms working to pull the T-shirt off over his head. It's hard not to be completely engrossed in his body as he drops the shirt to the floor, his toned abdomen and muscular arms distracting me as he begins to settle beside me once again.

"No, no, pants too." I gesture to the soaked jeans sticking to his legs and shake my head. He rolls his eyes but smirks as he peels the wet denim off his skin.

He drops them onto the floor with his shirt, and when he rolls back over to face me, his eyebrow isn't the only thing that's raised. "Better?"

"Better," I agree, staring at his large erection. I want to explore it, but he pulls me against his chest and smooths my hair with his hand.

"Walk first." He mumbles the reminder against my forehead, his hand absentmindedly beginning to run through my wavy strands. "Sleep, Flower."

"I still want to know what happened," I argue, pulling my gaze away from his cock so I can meet his gaze.

He's quiet for a moment as he contemplates his answer, then he sighs. "We're not sure what happened. Something tripped our alarm, but when we went to check it out, we couldn't find anything. It's probably just a malfunctioning wire or something."

I feel him shrug, but I can hear the uncertainty woven into his words.

They're not sure. It *could* be a broken wire, but it also *could* be something else.

"You worried me, you know." I run my fingers along the spot where I'd struck him, the skin still a slight pink from the blow. It's not bruised like I worried it would be, and I doubt that I'd ever be able to do any real damage if necessary. "You were all gone for so long... I wasn't sure who'd be coming through that door."

His arms tighten around me, a low hiss escaping through his teeth as if the thought of someone *else* finding me trapped in this room is enough to put him on edge. "If things got bad, I was going to come and get you out. We weren't going to let anything happen to you."

I knew when they left that they were storming out to fight whatever enemy they believed to be knocking on their front door, but I hadn't realized that while they were preparing for a fight, they were also worried about *me*.

"Do you really think it was a broken wire?" I whisper, studying his face.

He's chewing on the inside of his cheek, mulling over my question as he stares up at the ceiling.

"I don't know, Flower. I hope so." His eyes meet mine for a moment, and his hand lifts to gently stroke my cheek. "You look exhausted. You should try to get some sleep."

I know that he's trying to change the subject, and while I'm not ready to let the conversation shift, I can see that he's not ready to dive into the situation with me, yet. The questions I have can be answered later. I allow the room to fall silent around us, and my eyes to close, his cold limbs finally starting to warm around me. I have no intention of falling asleep beside him, but my orgasm and the whiskey still working through my system overthrow any predetermination I had made to stay awake. I'm drifting off before I have the foresight to fight it.

Chapter Fifteen

Xander

"It wasn't the wind. Someone *did* come over the wall." Everett's confirmation makes the hairs on the back of my neck stand, an unsettling chill spreading across my skin as he continues. "Whoever it was tripped the alarm while they were leaving."

I twist on the barstool I'm sitting on, turning away from the smooth wood of the workbench and my dismantled gun, to face him.

"Show me the footage." I can see the hesitation, the way his body naturally reacts to my command before his mind has the chance to override it, that dominant piece of himself unaccustomed to following someone else's orders.

He rolls his shoulders as he passes me the tablet, forcing his body to conform. "I'm not sure how they managed to get over without alerting us, but I've got a call out to have someone come and check the system tomorrow."

I play the video feed, watching over and over again as a hooded male figure climbs our cement wall and drops to the other side out of view, not a distinguishable feature in sight. Their face is obscured by a mask, and their body is concealed by dark, black clothing. The only thing that may be of some use to us, *if* we can get a clear view of the serial number, is a camera that dangles from a strap around their neck, the expensive-looking piece of technology dented and scratched.

Everett steps up beside me, waiting until I've watched through the footage again before reaching over and swiping to the side, loading a separate video from the camera out back. He hits play and watches with me as the man creeps through our backyard, the camera around his neck in the previous feed lifted to his eye and clutched tightly in his grasp. The bastard snaps a few photos and even takes the time to inspect his work on the digital image display on the back of the camera, a minuscule action that pisses me off to no end. He was so unafraid of being caught, on our *property*, that he took the time to check his handiwork.

"I can't be sure, but I think he's taking pictures of Brielle's room. Of us. I saw something out of the corner of my eye when we were with her, but I didn't think anything of it until you said something. He could've killed me." Everett mutters. His lips are pressed into a firm line, his body tense as we continue watching the feed. The man disappears into the expanse of foliage in our backyard, no doubt having spotted Everett at the window, and doesn't reappear for a few painstakingly long minutes. Eventually, the coward skitters out of his hiding spot to cross the lawn, a limp in his short, choppy stride. He makes quick work of pulling himself up and over the iron fence that closes in our backyard, the unpracticed motion revealing a gun, tucked into the waistband of his pants.

"If he came here with the intent to kill, he would've taken the shot while you were *distracted*." I thrust the tablet back into his hands. "He came here for information."

Everett's mouth parts, the beginning of a question forming on his tongue before he snaps his jaw shut, realization flooding his face. *That man came here for information on Brielle.*

"But...why?" He can't help but ask the one question I don't have the time or patience to have him figure out.

I push myself up, forgetting my gun on the workstation, and start toward the basement steps, cold and angry. If Brielle isn't already a part of our world, I've thrown her, headfirst and bleeding, into shark-infested waters by bringing her here. I've made her a target, someone our enemies can — and will — use to practice their proficiency.

"Where is Rhys?" I ask over my shoulder, stalling on the bottom step as Everett's face flashes with an unrecognizable emotion.

"With Brielle." It's in the tightness of his voice that I recognize the reaction that had momentarily crossed his face. *Jealousy.* I understand what's happened without him having to speak the words, and an annoyed sigh leaves my lips.

"Are they *done*?" I tighten my grip on the railing. He shrugs, his brown eyes rolling as he shuffles forward to follow me up the steps. "I want you to look through the footage and see if we missed anything else. I'm going to make a few calls and see if some of our men can scour the woods along our property line for anything that could lead us to our mystery man."

I catch his nod out of the corner of my eye as we reach the top of the steps, his fingers swiping along the tablet as he turns to disappear up the hall. I cross through the living room alone and climb the second set of stairs two at a time, intent on blowing past Brielle's room without a single glance in that direction until a sliver of light stops me in my tracks.

I scan the door — slightly ajar — easily spotting the hazel eyes that peer out at me through the gap.

"What are you doing?" I bark, watching as she nervously sucks in her bottom lip. I'm looming in the doorway, one hand locked on the wooden trim, the other tightly grasping the handle. *Did she think fucking my brother would help her escape?*

She swallows around the lump in her throat, a shaking hand pushing back the sweaty hair clinging to her forehead. "I — I was just going to get some water. Rhys fell asleep, and I — I didn't want to wake him."

Her voice wavers, and as she shifts on her feet, the nervousness of her actions pulls at something deep within me. My anger evaporates almost immediately, and a new feeling is quick to take root in its place.

"Let's go." I take a step back, releasing the door to allow her freedom as I turn to head back down the steps.

I'm halfway down when I hear her bare feet padding after me, the sound of them on the marble flooring causing a smile to grace my lips before I know what I'm doing. She's silent as she follows me, stopping at the edge of the kitchen to watch hesitantly as I pull an empty glass from one of the cabinets. I fill it with water from the fridge and slide it across the island, leaving it in front of a barstool with a single nod of invitation.

She's fumbling with the edge of the oversized shirt that she's wearing, but crosses the cool floor without hesitation, her small body lifting onto the barstool I've indicated as she grasps the glass of water with shaking hands.

"Are you all right?" The question surprises us both.

She freezes with her lips around the rim of the glass and takes a sip before lifting her steady gaze to meet mine. "I'm fine."

"You're shaking. I can't imagine sex with my brother was bad enough for you to—"

"I had a bad dream," she interrupts, her cheeks flushing at my insensitive jab.

She drops her gaze, choosing instead to scan the silent house, and I can see, even in the dim lighting, the bruises beginning to encircle her wrists. The sight curls my stomach into an uncomfortable knot, and it's not impossible to decipher the probable cause of her nightmares. *I'm sorry.* The words build on my tongue, but never make it past my lips. "About me?"

"No, Beast. Not about you." She's quick to respond, my god-forsaken nickname rolling off her tongue with a scowl. "It was about my mother."

Her mother. Although the Beaumont children were ghosts online, David had been able to scrounge up plenty of information on George's late wife after our little chat this morning. I haven't had the time to fully scour the report, but I've read enough to know that the woman died after a lengthy battle with cancer and on the night she died, Brielle was there with her brother. I never knew my mother, but I watched the life drain out of my father, a man I despised, and that was still difficult for me to digest. I can't imagine watching someone that you *love* die.

Again, those two words beg to spill into the silent air, but I ignore the urge and swallow them. I nod in the direction of the stairs and mutter with a firm growl, "You should get back upstairs before Rhys notices that you're gone."

"Yeah, I probably should," she agrees, finishing the last of her water before setting the empty glass back down on the counter.

She slips from the barstool, adjusts the men's sweats hanging from around her hips, and gives me one long, final look over her shoulder. There's a contemplative look there, her lips parted as if she wants to say more, before deciding better of it and sealing them shut. Her brown waves bounce against her back as she leaves without a second glance in my direction. *Fuck.*

I drop my head back and tug a hand through my beard, an annoyed grunt leaving me as I lean back against the counter. *How did I really expect that to go?* I offered no apology, no comfort when she was vulnerable with me. Goddamnit! *There are so many things that I need to apologize for but, where do I even begin...?*

If *I* put her in danger by bringing her into my home, then I'm going to have to stop acting like a child. I'll have to protect her from a world that I brought her into. I owe her that much.

Chapter Sixteen

Brielle

I don't sleep very well.

Despite the comfort Rhys' presence offers, I toss and turn for most of the night, my mind unwilling to settle long enough for me to get any real sleep. Between the nightmares of my mother and the unknown threat lurking over our heads, I can't fight the intrusive thoughts that keep me awake. When the sun is high enough in the sky to creep across the bedroom floor, Rhys rolls onto his side and wraps an arm around my waist.

"What's wrong, Flower?" He drags me into him, his green eyes foggy with the night's worth of missed sleep.

"I'm sorry. I didn't mean to keep you up," I whisper, pressing the heel of my hands into my heavy eyes with a sigh.

"I don't mind. Sure, I'd prefer we wasted our sleep in *other* ways, but…" He trails off with a light laugh, his thumb brushing my cheek. "Do you need to talk?"

"I think I just need some coffee," I mumble, my stomach growling at me as if the mere mention of caffeine is enough to wake my hunger.

He scans me, his eyebrows furrowing together above his sleepy eyes before he nods, knocking his messy hair loose around his face.

"I'll see what we've got for breakfast," he offers, pushing himself up. He bends down for his discarded clothes, but frowns, the fabric no doubt still damp from the downpour he walked through last night. He leaves them on the floor and straightens, his arms stretched above his head as he yawns. "I should probably get dressed first. I'll see if I can rustle up something less…*masculine* for you."

I shake my head as he winks, his nearly bare body halfway out of the door when he stops abruptly. I sit up, tossing the warm comforter off my legs as I try to see around him. "What is it?"

"It's an outfit for you," he replies, bending forward to pick the neat pile of clothes up off the floor. He grins as he inspects them, his tired eyes warming with heat as he looks between me and the clothing in his hands. He takes a few steps to the side, drops them onto the nearby chair then heads back toward the door once more. "I'll meet you downstairs, Flower."

"Wait, who would—" He disappears before the question makes it past my lips, an irritated groan leaving me as my feet sink into the carpet. *Why can't I choose my own damn clothes?* I roll my eyes as I cross the room, unsure of the heated look behind Rhys' gaze as I pick up the fabric. They look normal to me—a red long-sleeved top and blue jeans with white sneakers tucked underneath, but I'm quick to realize what's missing from the pile. *Underwear.*

"Fuckers," I mutter, my eyes bouncing around the room until I spot the ruined pair lying torn and discarded on the carpet. *I guess I'm going commando.*

Leaving behind the shoes, I walk into the en suite and set the clothes on the vanity then turn on the hot water for a quick shower. I wash up, carefully rinsing my sensitive core, before slipping from the pristine shower stall and drying off. I pull on the jeans, the material conforming to my figure, and stare down in shock at the holes carved into the soft, expensive fabric. More than half of my upper right leg is exposed by a large split gaping the fabric, and another, smaller rip shows my lower thigh and knee. *My ruined jeans hide more skin than this!* I guess I could try to find whatever drawer Mrs. Claebourne stashed them away in, but I'd be lying if I said my stomach wasn't twisting in anticipation at the thought of wearing these for them. *Fuck it.*

I lift the shirt to slip it on and see that it's completely backless, a thin strap of material the only thing keeping the piece together. *I guess I'm going braless, too.*

"I am going to kill them." Even as the words leave my lips, a dampness begins to form between my legs, betraying my buried desires before I'm ready to acknowledge them.

I can curse, scream, and threaten them all I want. Truth be told, if I *really* didn't want this, I'd slip back into the clothes on the bathroom floor. No, I *want* to look sexy for them…and damn whichever brother made me realize it.

I pull on the shirt before turning to inspect my exposed back, smiling at the way the red color complements my complexion. It's the first piece of red clothing that I've worn in a long time, and the color does nothing to conceal my figure like I'd normally prefer. When I turn back around, my nipples are on full display, the coldness of the room making them pebble against the fabric. *If they want a show, I'll give them a show.*

I thrust my shoulders back and lift my chin, crossing toward the chair where I pick up the white sneakers. I'm about to sit down and slip them on when I spot a black hair tie resting on the chair, previously unnoticed by the distraction of my missing undergarments. *They want an unencumbered view...*

A shiver of excitement tears through me as I tie my hair back into a messy bun, a few shorter tendrils falling free as I slip on the shoes.

"Confidence, Brielle. Confidence." I whisper words of encouragement to myself as I stand and open the unlocked bedroom door. I don't hesitate to move into the hall, my shoes squeaking on the stairs as I make my way down.

"Fucking hell." Rhys groans. He's sitting in the kitchen, his green eyes devouring me as I round the corner into the living room.

Xander is sitting with him at the island, his black curls restrained in a tight knot, his large arms on display in the gray T-shirt he's wearing. It's the first time I've seen him without sleeves, his tan skin coated in black swells of ink that dance along the curves of his muscles and stop at the base of his wrists. I'm so lost in the designs that I almost miss the smirk on his lips.

"Was it you this time?" I question, stopping beside him as he openly scans me.

He growls out a breath, his jaw tense as he takes in my figure, his fingers stretching and pressing into the tops of his thighs.

"No, Princess. I don't pick out clothes for women, I take them off." He swallows, a rough exhale breaking past his sealed lips that makes my legs shake unsteadily.

"Everett did this?" I question, chewing on my lower lip.

"Why do you sound so surprised?" Everett's voice makes me jump, his calloused fingers skating down the exposed skin of my back.

I whirl around to face him, gasping at his closeness, and shiver as his hands grip the counter on either side of me, bracketing me in place. I guess I *shouldn't* be surprised. These men have proven more than once that they enjoy keeping me on my toes, and I need to stop expecting less. He leans into me, the scent of his aftershave overpowering the mixed aromas filling the kitchen as his smooth cheek brushes against mine.

"Your moans drove me mad last night, pet." He grabs a cup of coffee off the counter behind me and steps back, his brown eyes swirling with heat as he smirks down at me. "I couldn't sleep."

I can feel a flush of color warming my neck and cheeks. *I kept them both up last night, and I'm not the tiniest bit sorry.*

I turn away from him to face the counter again, a smile on my lips as I reach across the island to grab my own mug of espresso. "So, what's for breakfast?"

Rhys laughs, but the sound is cut off by a screech that nearly makes me drop my mug, my heart leaping into my throat as my eyes search to find the source of the unexpected noise. Mrs. Claebourne is hovering in the doorway, her coat clutched in a tight fist as she gestures wildly toward the living room floor.

"Well? What is this mess?" She frowns, her angry eyes scanning the boys.

I lift onto my toes, peering over the back of the couch so that I can see the mess that she's describing, and find a trail of muddy footprints that track from the back door down the hall.

"Mrs. Claebourne —"

"Don't you start with me, Xander! Do you know how difficult it is for me to get on my knees and clean up a mess like this?" she scolds, crossing her arms over her chest. "Don't think for a moment that you can blame this on your brothers, I know these are your footprints."

I can't suppress my giggle, the sound of it causing Xander's head to snap in my direction, his eyebrows furrowed in anger. "What's so funny, Princess?"

"You, being scolded like a toddler," I whisper, overly confident as I press my fingers to my lips.

"Xander —"

"We'll get it cleaned up, Mrs. Claebourne," Everett interjects, interrupting Claire before she has the chance to further rebuke his brother.

Her steely gaze rakes over each of them, her frustrated expression only softening so she can shoot a warm smile in my direction. "I'll get started upstairs."

She leaves, moving on feet more graceful than my own. *How old is she, anyway?*

"I've got to get to work. I want an update as soon as you have it." Xander pushes away his empty mug and stands, waiting until his brothers have nodded their understanding before disappearing from the room.

Once he's gone, Everett presses a hand to my lower back and sets a plate of food down in front of the now vacated seat. "You need to learn to stop poking the Beast."

He gestures for me to sit, and I'm quick to lift myself into the chair, sipping from my coffee as I release a long sigh. Again, I'm not sorry.

"Does he actually have work, or is he just trying to get out of cleaning the floors?" I ask.

"We *do* have real jobs, ya know. Not respectable ones, but jobs nonetheless." Rhys chuckles, plopping into the chair beside me.

He's made omelets, stuffed with fresh vegetables, cheese and bacon, the smell enough to make my mouth water.

"We'll have to take her on an *outing* one day." Everett smirks, an inside joke passing between the two men. I frown, wanting to ask what they mean, but Everett presses a fork into my hand, distracting me. "Eat, pet."

The new nickname he's curated for me makes my breath catch, the excitement and sudden need to please him driving me to shovel a large bite of food into my mouth. His approving nod makes me squirm, a breathy whimper leaving me that makes Rhys chuckle from beside me. What kind of unexplored desire is *this*?

"I should probably swing by the office today, too. Will you two be okay on your own?" Rhys asks, his fingers skating along my exposed thigh.

"We'll be fine." Everett nods, stealing a bite of food off my plate. "Other than the system check, my schedule is wide open."

System check? I glance between the two of them skeptically but find myself nodding anyway, somehow realizing that, even if I ask, I won't be getting any of the answers to my questions. *I'll have to figure out what's going on, on my own.* Whether they want me to or not.

Chapter Seventeen

Xander

Brielle Beaumont is going to break me.

After years of being beaten down and taught to live without attachments, without emotions, that woman is making me feel *alive* again.

My feet are unsteady as I pace the bedroom floor, unable to get the image of her in that red shirt out of my head, my dick straining against my jeans. I'd like to believe that it's just lust that she's ignited and sent boiling through my veins, but try as I might, I can't ignore the truth. Her teasing demeanor and her lighthearted laughter made me *happy*. When was the last time someone was able to curb my anger like she did, so easily?

I pull my fingers through my hair, yanking it free of the tie restraining it and stomp toward the bathroom, needing to numb the pain threatening to crack my chest wide open. I strip out of my clothes, my erect cock springing free as I turn on the shower and step inside, the lukewarm water making me groan. *Not cold enough.* I twist the handle, turning the spray into an icy rain that chills me to the bone, my teeth grinding as I welcome the sharp sting that works its way across my skin. *I can't feel...beasts don't feel.* I press my hand against the shower wall, flashbacks threatening to break down the walls I've built to conceal them as water pounds against my ruined back.

"What did I say?" My father's phantom voice screams in my ear, the snap of his belt echoing through my head so real I tense in preparation for the blow. *"Tears don't earn sympathy, they earn pain!"*

I shudder, bile burning my throat as the memory of that day churns my stomach, the recollection of the blood spilled from my body and the stitches I'd had to sit through, unmedicated, making me ill. I vomit, dropping to my knees on the shower floor as I retch, my liquid breakfast sloshing along the shower floor as I shake, my eyes squeezed shut. *Stop feeling!* I breathe, forcing back the memories and emotions, willing myself to forget, *needing* to forget...

I stay seated on the cold tiled floor with my head under the water until the memories have passed, slipping and disappearing down the drain with the water cascading off my body. Eventually, I allow myself to reach up and shut it off, my fingers and toes numb as I lift myself to my feet and wrap a towel around my waist. I stumble forward, my curls dripping water down my back as I lean against the vanity, my eyes scanning myself in the mirror.

The black ink covering my skin doesn't hide the redness that's developed from the cold, and although the designs are meant to camouflage the scarring left behind by my father, they don't distract from them completely. While most of the damage is on my back, an assortment of burns and cuts decorate my upper body in a mismatched collage of betrayal that sets my teeth on edge.

"Beast...?"

I tense, that nickname coming from *her* lips adding to the pain that's spiraling through me. *Why won't she let me be numb?* Doesn't she realize? Feeling only brings more *pain.*

"What're you doing in here, Princess?" I growl, my shoulders tensing with rage. I can see her hovering in the bathroom doorway, her wide eyes filled with tears as she takes a hesitant step toward me. "Get the fuck *out.*"

"Xander—"

"Go! Leave!" I scream, my anger exploding, rising to protect me from the pain I've grown to anticipate after succumbing to weaknesses like the emotions tearing through me. I advance on her, the threat of my size causing her to stumble backward, her face paling in fear. "Get out of here!"

My roar makes the hairs on my own arms stand, but despite her evident panic, and the tears beginning to track down her face, she doesn't run. Her hand reaches forward to gently caress a scar puckering the skin of my left arm, the touch detonating the bomb already ticking in my chest. I shatter, my fear taking over.

I yell.

I scream.

I curse her as I move, throwing on clothes to keep her eyes off my broken body. She watches silently, frozen against the wall I'd nearly pushed her against until I'm dressed and heaving in front of her. I can see the confusion in her torn expression, the desperation and desire to help, but I *can't* let her in. I can't be *weak*.

I grab her hand and tug her toward the bedroom door, still breathing hard as I snatch my gun off the nearby table. She's tense, but she doesn't object as I lead her through the house, down the stairs, and into the foyer, where Everett and a technician are working.

"Beast? What's going—"

I usher Brielle through the side door and into the garage before he has the chance to finish, my free hand slamming the door as realization dawns on his face. He knows.

I am going to finish this.

Chapter Eighteen

Brielle

What was I thinking?

I swipe away the last of my tears and tuck my chin, my breath clouding in the air as I step off the side of the road, desperate to catch my breath. *What was I thinking…?*

"It doesn't matter. None of it matters, now." I tread through the throng of overgrowth to hide within the coverage of trees, my white sneakers sinking into the wet earth beneath me. I can't risk being spotted by one of the other brothers. Not until I've decided what I'm going to do. Yes, I'm free, but instead of the excitement and joy I'd thought I'd feel, I just feel…*regret.*

After Xander all but threw me into the passenger seat of his car, we drove for a few miles before he pulled us over onto the shoulder of the deserted road, his face impassive and unreadable. I was prepared for the worst, for his gun to be drawn and aimed between my unexpecting eyes, but he'd simply leaned across me and opened the door. *"Get out."* The order was muttered so quietly it was almost a plea, his face contorted as I unbuckled my seatbelt and slipped from the car. I watched him drive off, my heart sinking as I realized that, somewhere in the last few days, I'd managed to forget one crucial and devastating detail — I was just their *prisoner*. It would never matter how well they treat me, their kindness would never amount to the freedom they'd stolen or would *continue* to hold, just out of my reach if I went back. *Why am I stalling?* Why am I hesitating, while my one chance at retaking that freedom hovers in front of me, fading with each passing moment? I *have* to keep going.

"I have to go home," I whisper, hoping that by saying the words, I can urge myself forward.

It doesn't work. My feet remain cemented in place as my mind wanders back to the three mysterious men, my two wants and desires splitting me in half. I can't ignore the connection I feel with Rhys or the fiery draw that lures me to Everett. Even beneath our combative personalities, I can feel something pulling me toward Xander, a need and drive to help him release the inner demons he's so obviously battling. That's all I'd wanted when I stumbled into his room and discovered the damage hiding beneath his tattoos. To help him.

But he turned on me, his eyes so black with anger that I didn't have any choice but to go with him.

So I followed him, silently, complacently.

And now I'm here.

I wrap my arms around myself, the chill in the air biting through my thin shirt and making me shiver. Beneath the trees, the small amount of sunlight that manages to reach the ground isn't enough to warm the ache beginning to grow in my bones. I want to get back on the road, to walk with the warm pavement beneath my feet, but I know that if I *truly* do not want to go back, I'll need to stay hidden. *Maybe they won't come for me.* I'm sure Xander is relieved to have me out of his hair, but the look Everett had shot me before I'd been ushered past him, his conversation with that stranger cutting off, was nothing short of fear. Fear of losing me? Maybe. Fear of Xander's resounding anger? Definitely. Would he risk that to come after me?

"Brielle? Brielle Beaumont?" A man's voice makes me jump, my surprised gasp echoing through the otherwise quiet woods as I whirl around to face the unexpected intrusion.

A stranger is climbing out of the passenger seat of a car, his face a battered discoloration of features that makes me wince and take a startled step back.

"Who are you?" My voice quivers, from the cold or fear, I'm unsure.

I've seen and treated worse injuries in my time at school, but beneath his broken body and outward injuries, I can sense something…dark. It's putting me on edge, the sinister look in his eyes almost familiar. *Why do I recognize him?*

"Your father sent us. He hired us to bring you home." His words take a moment to register, the uncanny feeling in my stomach too much of a distraction. My *father* sent him?

The man is closing the distance between us now, and two additional men are snaking from the car to follow him, leaving only one set of dark eyes to watch me from the rolled-down window of their vehicle.

"Hired you?" I swallow around the lump in my throat and scan them, their impassive faces only aiding the panic swelling in my gut.

My father couldn't hire a doctor to care for my mother, his *wife*, when she was dying. After accumulating a mountain of debt for her treatments, and my schooling, how would he afford a team of men to rescue me?

The man on the left smiles at my confusion, his head swiveling to the side so he can hiss something to the others, and it's in that small flick of his neck that I catch a glimpse of the tattoo inked onto his flesh there. *A wolf.*

Run.

I turn, prepared to take off, but a rough hand latches onto my upper arm and yanks, the force of the pull nearly enough to knock me to the ground. "You're coming with us, sweetheart."

I only glance up enough to see the mangy dog etched onto his skin before I swing my fist up, aiming for his nose. My knuckles connect with cartilage, a sickening crunch erupting from the man's face before his steely grip around my arm breaks, allowing me to twist out of his grasp.

Shouts rise through the trees as I take off, my feet pounding into the mud beneath me as I run. They are quick to follow me, their long legs bringing them to me before I have the chance to create any true distance between us. Fingers snag my hair before I can react, a splitting pain erupting through my skull as they rip me to a stop, my scalp burning as I'm forced to my knees in front of them.

"Easy, now. The boss won't want her marked up," the battered man grunts, his slow lumbering stride finally bringing him to us. He's short, maybe only a few inches taller than me, and his hair and skin are slicked with enough sweat that he's shining in the dim lighting. He eyes the two men hovering above me, a cruel smile curling his lips as he nods down in my direction with a gruff growl. "Take what you're owed so we can get out of here."

"I—I was just their prisoner... They won't come for me," I grit out, whimpering as the man behind me yanks at my hair again and hisses at me to keep quiet.

If these men think that they're going to be able to use me to hurt the Grimm Brothers, they're just as confused about our relationship as I am. They're not going to get anywhere using me as bait. May as well kill me now to save themselves the trouble.

"She's really got no idea, does she?" The man I'd struck earlier squats down in front of me, blood pooling from his broken nose in waves that drip onto his plain T-shirt. His eyes are dark, his pupils dilated enough to swallow the soulless brown color that rims his irises, and I shift uncomfortably beneath his gaze.

His hand snaps forward so quickly that I don't have time to react, pain splintering across my cheek as he makes contact, the blow knocking my head to the side with a scream.

"We'll tell him the brothers roughed her up a bit to save us the hassle of being gentle." He pinches my chin between his thumb and index finger, his touch making the hairs on my arms stand as he forces my gaze back to him, his laughter spilling across my heated face. His yellow, plaque-covered teeth are on display as he smiles, his tongue darting out to swipe up the blood that's collected along his top lip with a moan. "Just a bit of payback, sweetheart."

His hand moves up to roughly squeeze my jaw, his nails biting into my skin as he stands, forcing my head back further with a sickening grin that makes my body freeze over. My stomach twists, realization souring the food in my gut. *Take what you're owed.* The words echo through my head. He's going to let them *use* me...as payment.

"P-Please, let me go." The plea sounds pathetic, even to me, my words breaking as I quiver.

He doesn't pause, reaching toward his fly as I thrash, uncaring as nails and hands tear into me, a loud cry escaping my sealed lips as the two men struggle to keep me still in front of them. The greasy, battered man has backed off, choosing instead to watch from a distance as the man behind me accepts his prior invitation and lowers himself to the ground, his hands reaching around me to fondle my unprotected chest. He gropes me, his free hand pinching at my breasts as I writhe, my fists pounding into the thighs of the monster in front of me as he successfully yanks his zipper down.

I'm sobbing, tears flowing down my face before I have the chance to stop them, another scream bubbling in my throat as my hair is released, only to have an arm yanked behind me instead. I let the sound lash from my throat, but if it weren't for the scratching feeling left behind in its wake, I would've never known the noise made it past my lips.

A gunshot erupts through the clearing, drowning out my voice and stalling the hands that hold me. Blood rains down on me, a copper mist that splatters along my face and clothes, before the man in front of me crumples to reveal a familiar form hovering across the clearing.

"Beast...?"

He came back.

He came back for *me*.

"Amour!" he calls to me, the new nickname rolling off his tongue before his shout morphs into a pained grunt, his body whirling around to face the man that's snuck up behind him.

I recognize him as the man that they'd left behind with the car, and watch helplessly as a fight ensues, metal flashing and arms flailing. The battered man, seizing the opportunity the fight creates, runs away. He darts toward the trees, sprinting as fast as his injuries will allow back toward the road as Xander tosses his combatant away with a shout.

"Beast!" I call, yanking at my arm, attempting to free myself from the man still restraining me.

He releases me with a low growl, the hands that had pinched and groped at me now mindlessly reaching for my shirt as he stands, intent on yanking me up with him and instead only ripping at the tie securing my shirt. I turn to scramble away from him and the bloodied body lying in front of me, but a booted foot swings into my side, crumpling me and rendering me useless as he stomps off toward Xander, metal glinting in his grasp.

My world spins, black splotches distorting my vision as pain crushes the air from my lungs. I'm paralyzed, frozen in place as I try to breathe, pain splintering through my chest and back. *Broken ribs.* Untreatable, but not life-threatening, not like the man that lies beside me, who's somehow beginning to move. *He's not dead.* I scream out a mangled cry as his sweaty hand grasps my wrist, tugging at me angrily, roughly, while the other reaches for the weapon exposed at his side.

I pull out of his grasp, gagging as blood sputters from his lips and pools from the gaping hole in his chest. I scoot back, grunting as pain sparks through my ribs, my entire body recoiling as another gunshot rips through the still air. *Who won?* I'm too weak, too scared to look across the clearing. Will it be Xander's blood staining the grass red? Will it be his body lying lifeless and defeated while these men take me? The thought almost makes me laugh, hysteria creeping over me as I realize that I've traded one prison for another. A *worse* one.

I flinch as another gunshot rings out, my hands pressing to my ears in an attempt to silence the ringing reverberating through my head. I don't realize that I've squeezed my eyes shut until the light stroke of a thumb against my raw cheek makes me jump.

"Amour, look at me." Xander's broken voice is quiet, a mixture of pain and concern lacing his demand as the light touch against my skin evaporates, the glancing brush so quick I'm not even sure it was real. Reluctantly, I peel my eyes open, my lips trembling as I take him in. My captor, my savior, kneeling in front of me covered in another man's blood. "Are you hurt?"

I shake my head, afraid that if I try to speak even that small confirmation, my voice will fail me. He nods and tilts his chin away, his jaw clenched so tightly that I worry his teeth might shatter as he begins to unbutton his shirt. I'm not sure what he's doing, wincing and grunting in pain as he shrugs off the bloody fabric, until he drapes it over my shoulders. It's only then that I realize my shirt is ruined, the fabric hanging around my body and leaving me exposed. I flush, embarrassed, and quickly work to clasp his shirt around me. I don't have the chance to thank him.

His large body sways, and he collapses, his normally tan face pale and clammy. I lean over him, assessing him for injuries, panic creeping into my bones as I notice the blood staining through his undershirt. I reach out, my fingers about to brush his chest when I freeze, a selfish piece of me screaming. *I could run.* I could race home to my family and try to leave this part of my life behind…but he would die.

"Dammit, Beast." I bite back the sting of pain that comes as I peel up his shirt, the door of my freedom slamming shut as I spot the cause of his bleeding. A shallow stab wound is allowing blood to spill from his body, an injury that could become deadly if I don't find help soon.

I rip off the bottom hem of his shirt, and use the fabric to pack the wound, one hand working to apply pressure while the other checks his pulse. It's steady, and a small sigh of relief leaves me as his eyes slowly flutter open.

"Beast, we need help. Do you have a phone? Can we call one of your brothers?" I pat him down, searching his pockets for a cell, but I only find his gun, still warm from use.

"It's i-in the car," he mutters, his teeth grinding as I press harder against his wound, the fabric already beginning to soak with his blood. *I can't leave him.* The last time that I left someone behind they *died.*

"You have to get up, I can't—I can't carry you." I don't hide the panic that's crept into my voice, the trauma of losing my mother filling me with worry as his face continues to lose its color. "Please, Beast. I just need you to get to the car."

My fear seems to stir him. He nods and sits, a curse leaving him as he grips my hand, helping apply pressure to the wound as he forces his feet beneath him. He stands, and I lay one of his arms over my shoulders, attempting to support some of his weight as he takes a staggering step forward.

I turn, intent on scanning the surrounding area, but Xander pulls me into him with a rough shake of his head. "Don't look, Amour. Don't torture yourself. I can lead us back."

"Why did you kill them?" I'm whispering the question before I realize what I'm saying, my eyes on our hands as he slowly leads us forward.

"I could have, and *should* have done much worse for what they were going to do to you." He growls, his merciless voice dripping with venom as his hand tightens around mine. "Killing them was a nicety they didn't deserve."

I can't find the words or the drive to argue with him, my soul darkening as I realize with a wince that I'm *grateful* for their deaths.

What kind of person does that make me...?

Chapter Nineteen

Everett

"What the hell happened?" It's the third time I've asked, my eyes following Brielle's blood-covered hands as she works to patch up a stab wound on Xander's abdomen, her entire frame engulfed by his oversized shirt.

She's coated in blood, thick clumps of it matting her hair and drying along her skin, her plump lips pressed into a thin line as she continues to avoid my gaze. *Something is wrong.* While the bruise beginning to form on her cheek and the nail marks torn into her skin appear to be her only wounds, I can see in the skittish way she moves that there's damage far beyond these surface injuries.

I want somebody's fucking head. "Who did this?"

"The Wolves," Xander grits out.

He's losing blood quicker than his body can replenish it, and while the loss in volume is making him ill, the stubborn bastard still hasn't passed out. He vomits into a nearby trash can I set up for him before collapsing back against the couch, growling as Brielle presses a fresh pad against his wound. She winces, recoiling before she can catch herself, a small curse leaving her lips as her eyes finally lift to meet mine.

"Did you call the doctor?" she whispers the first words I've heard her speak since our conversation this morning.

When I saw Xander hauling her off, I wanted to go after them, but he was too quick. By the time I'd grabbed my keys, scrambled into a car, and raced down the driveway, they were gone. There was nothing left I could do but *hope* that she'd changed him enough to survive. When I saw a call coming in from him fifteen minutes later, I wasn't sure what to expect. It certainly didn't occur to me that Brielle could be on the other end, calling for *help*.

"Yes, he's on the way." I nod, watching helplessly as she struggles to bandage his bleeding wound.

Xander has *never* been injured like this in a fight, and the sight of him, grumbling and groaning beneath Brielle's touch, makes my chest tighten in anger. As soon as she's repacked the laceration, she turns her attention to the other wounds decorating his chest, an array of slash marks he must have received during the brawl, and cleans those, too.

"You should've let me take you to the hospital. If he doesn't bring a suture kit, you'll bleed out before an ambulance can get here." Brielle shakes her head, tucking her lip between her teeth as Xander lets out a labored groan in response, his eyes flicking up to mine for a fleeting moment before they drop back to the girl shivering beside him.

What the fuck happened?

"They're right in here." Mrs. Claebourne's worried voice floats into the room as she leads Dr. Patel into the house, his salt-and-pepper hair pushed back over his head.

"What happened?" he asks the question I'm still waiting for an answer to, his hands pulling on a pair of gloves as he kneels beside Brielle.

"He was stabbed. There's a two or three-inch jagged laceration to his left lower quadrant." Brielle rattles off a list of symptoms and probable blood loss before allowing Dr. Patel the needed room to work, his hands quick to peel back the gauze so he can assess the damage.

"You're one lucky bastard, Mr. Grimm. You shouldn't need anything too extensive, thanks to this one." He nods toward Brielle and leans over to grab some items from his bag, allowing the conversation to drop as he gets to work.

This is one of the many reasons I've always insisted on keeping an emergency physician on our payroll — they're smart, which means they know enough to keep us alive, while also knowing better than to pry into our affairs.

"I'll go upstairs and make sure his room is ready for him. Please excuse me." Mrs. Claebourne's wrinkled face is marred with concern, and her normally pink-tinged cheeks have lost their color.

The old woman has never had much of a tolerance for blood, especially where we're concerned, so I'm not surprised to hear that she's running off to find something to distract her. My eyes drift to Brielle, who's quietly watching Dr. Patel's steady hands as they suture Xander's side, her own wringing in her lap, and know that *she* needs a distraction, too.

"Come on, pet. Let's get you cleaned up." Her eyes fly to me, her face heating at the nickname I've used before she looks back to Xander.

He's got one large arm tossed over his eyes, his teeth grinding together as the doc threads a needle into his flesh, the pain meds he'd agreed to take still needing time to work.

"Go on, Amour," Xander grumbles, his chest rising and falling in quick, uneven movements.

I can see the discomfort layered within his tense posture, and while I'm sure *some* of it is from the pain, I know him well enough to see the real cause of his misery. He *hates* weakness. I'm sure that lying here, having Brielle look after him while he's suffering, is only aiding the battle waging within his twisted head, so—while I know he'll never say it—I think he's grateful for the opportunity to be alone.

"What about Rhys...?" The question falls from her lips as she stands, her arms wrapping protectively around herself as she steps up beside me.

"I called him, too. I'm sure he'll come to find us when he gets back," I tell her, leading her toward the stairs.

She falls into step behind me, her eyes glued to the floor as if she's afraid it'll move out from under her if she's not watching it. When we reach the top step she turns to the left, heading for her room, but I hook an arm around her waist and guide her in the opposite direction, shrugging at the questioning look she shoots me. With everything that's happened today and the mystery man that was snapping photos of her bedroom last night, I'm *not* ready to let her go in there just yet. Not until I've had the chance to scope the property and check the live feed, and I can't do that until Rhys gets back. *I can't leave her alone.*

I pull her into my bedroom, lowering my arm from around her so that I can shut the door behind us. Her curious gaze flicks around the space, undoubtedly noting that this is the sparsest room in our home before her attention floats back to me. She looks otherworldly, a pale ghost with death reflected on her stained skin. I can see the pain in her haunting gaze and a desperation words can't explain locked deep within it.

"What do you need, Brielle?" My voice is low as I watch her struggle, her internal battle almost palpable in the silent room.

The look she gives me is a mixture of a thousand different emotions, her brow furrowing as she attempts to form her needs into words. I watch as each emotion battles to take hold and claim victory over her waning control, her fists pressing into her eyes.

"I—I can't—" She lets out a sharp breath. "I need to feel something else. *Anything* else."

I take the two steps needed to bring me to her, my hands gently landing on either side of her face. She peeks up at me from behind her fists as my thumbs stroke her bruising cheeks, racing over the nail marks torn into her skin. *We both need this distraction.*

"Gentle or rough, pet. What side of me do you need right now?" I ask with a growl, trying to swallow back the surge of need that's beginning to course through me.

"Rough." She doesn't pause to allow herself time to think, her confident response providing some relief to the worry attempting to drown me.

I don't hesitate. I race my hands down her body, ignoring the blood that's coating her, and drop my eyes to the clothes still concealing her from me.

"Take off your pants," I order, smiling at the way she shivers at the command. "I'm going to show you what happens when you break my rules, pet."

"I'm sorry, sir." Her apology is betrayed by the heat in her eyes, a hunger bubbling to life as she unbuttons her jeans and slips them down her toned legs. Her tongue darts out as she stands, wetting her dry lips, and I curse, my teeth grinding as I catch a glimpse of her bare, shaved pussy.

"Fuck, pet." I'm *so* glad I didn't give her underwear this morning. I try to rein in what little control I have over myself, but her teasing glances and dangerous words have my cock hardening in my jeans. "Before we go any further, you need to know our safe words. You can say these to my brothers or me, and we'll understand and adjust accordingly. Red makes everything stop, no hesitations, no guilt. Yellow means that you're close to your breaking point and are starting to get uncomfortable. If you say it, we'll stop and see if you're okay to keep going and make any necessary adjustments. Do you understand?"

She nods but must realize that I'm looking for a verbal agreement because she breathes out a quick and simple, "Yes."

I stalk across the room, smirking at her dissatisfied whimper as I pass her, reminding myself to move slow as I lower myself onto the edge of the bed. I adjust myself, uncaring of the eyes lingering on my bulge. "I'm going to spank you for misbehaving, pet. Come here and accept your punishment."

Chapter Twenty

Brielle

He's going to spank me?

I stifle the moan that attempts to escape me at the thought, my thighs pressing together in a failed attempt at relieving the pressure that's building between them. This is a dangerous game that we're playing, and I know that we're crossing a line. I'm digging myself deeper into the hole I've fallen into, but for some reason, I can't stop myself from inching toward him, an overwhelming need driving me forward. I have to feel something other than the guilt, fear, anger and sadness that's ripping me apart, but will the pain he's offering be the solution I'm searching for? I'm breaking so many rules, lusting after not one, but *two* of my captors, but I need them, I need *this*, to keep me grounded.

I stop a few steps short of Everett, unapologetically taking him in as he watches me and waits for me to make the first move. He's not as muscular as Xander, or as lean as Rhys, but a mixture of them both that makes him more dangerous—more lethal. People probably underestimate him based on his outward appearance alone, foolishly ignoring the loyalty that lies at his core. That loyalty, the need to protect and defend those that he loves, is the reason that he's built the muscles on his arms. Or, maybe, it was to punish *misbehaving women.* I scan his large hands, calloused and rough, and imagine how they'll feel against my backside, striking me to punish and pleasure. Will I like it?

I close the space left between us, my breath catching in my throat as he reaches out to stroke my thigh, his heated brown eyes locked on mine as his lips pull into a slow grin.

"Bend over, pet." His instructions make my knees buckle, a fresh wave of desires I'd never imagined washing over me.

I swallow back the uncertainty that attempts to force me to retreat and step in front of him, turn, and bend over as far as my ribs will allow. The air licks up my exposed center as he pushes the tail of Xander's shirt out of the way, a low groan leaving his throat as he caresses the skin where my ass and thighs meet appreciatively. "Tell me why you're being punished."

I release my swollen lower lip, wriggling in front of him as he continues to caress the soft, exposed flesh at his mercy, a dampness beginning to grow between my legs.

"I put myself in danger?" I question, anticipation swelling in my gut. What could this possibly feel like?

"*Unnecessary* danger," he corrects with a growl, pulling back and snapping his palm across my bottom. I squeak, a delicious wave of heat sparking up my core as he rubs away the sting. "You're ours, Brielle. Ours to destroy, and to claim. You should've come back home."

His possessive words don't have time to register before another strike snaps against my skin, hitting the same location so that the residual pain increases, an unexpected moan escaping my lips. *Oh. I do like this...*

His hand slips between my legs, a hissed curse leaving him as he finds the dampness soaking my inner thighs, his fingers running along my wet center. "Grab your calves, pet."

I'm quick to follow his directions, enjoying the praise he murmurs to me at my compliance, and wrap my hands around my legs, shifting my weight from foot to foot as I wait for the next strike to land.

Without warning, he slips a digit into me, a warm sensation flooding my body as he curls and brushes a tangled bundle of nerves deep within me, pulling a soft gasp past my parted lips. I push back, wanting *more* of that feeling, groaning and whimpering as another strike lands with a sharp rush of pain against my ass. *Oh my god.* He smacks me again, his finger slipping in and out of my pussy simultaneously, the mixture of sensations causing a warmth to spread in my stomach. He grips my raw flesh, rubbing in the sting as he slips in and out of my soaking cunt, his thumb circling my clit and tossing me forward in a race toward ecstasy.

"Fuck, Everett!" I cry out as he spanks me again, striking with precision, the pain and pleasure intermixing as he slips another finger into me with ease.

Unencumbered moans rise from me as I bounce against his fingers, chasing the orgasm I can feel building, blooming, and finally crashing around me. I can't contain my cries of pleasure as I melt, my body quaking as his fingers continue to work, stroking me until I've resurfaced, exhausted and weak, on the other side of my release. He slips his fingers from me, reaching around me to pull me down into his lap, his eyebrows raising as he studies me with a grin.

"I'm glad you enjoyed your punishment, pet, but be warned…the next time you misbehave, I will not be so forgiving." His steely warning makes a shiver race up my spine, a mischievous part of me already beginning to plot and scheme possible ways to get him to bend me over again.

He raises a brow, as if able to read my mind, and a bout of laughter swells in my stomach. My hand flies up to conceal the noise and I catch a glimpse of the blood still staining my skin. I freeze, my laughter cutting off as a sickening feeling pops the euphoric bubble I'd been floating in.

Back to reality, Brielle.

I drop my hand, my lips pressing into a thin line as I glance back up at Everett, hating the concern and worry I can see clouding his gaze. He opens his mouth, that damned question forming on his lips again, the question that will make me remember, so I shake my head, silently begging him not to ask. *I don't want to go back.* "Can I shower, please?"

He nods despite his need for answers and allows me to slip from his lap, his eyes trailing over me as I tug at the edge of the shirt. He's slow to push himself to his feet behind me, a sad sigh leaving him as he turns to lead me toward the en suite. The bathroom is identical to mine, aside from the toiletries that fill the space, but Everett still turns on the shower and adjusts the heat for me. He grabs a fresh towel and sets it on the counter before crossing back toward me, his hands gently lifting to grip the shirt still covering me. He tips up a brow, and although a larger part of me wants to be alone, I can't ignore the smaller side of me that wants to be taken care of. I nod, watching as he works to unfasten the buttons securing the shirt, my face flushing as he takes in the ruined shirt underneath. He bites back a growl as he helps me out of that one, too. I thought I'd feel embarrassed, or at least shy, standing in front of him naked for the first time, but after the moment we just shared, I feel comfortable and *safe*.

"Brielle..." He trails off, his throat constricting as he swallows, his large eyes heated with anger as his fingers skate along my right side. I flinch. "I'm so—"

"Don't," I whisper, interrupting him with a quick shake of my head. Just like I wouldn't allow Rhys to apologize for Xander's mistakes, I won't allow Everett to apologize for this. *It isn't his fault.*

I twist away from him, needing to inspect the damage, and scan my reflection in the mirror. It's not hard to spot the bruise beginning to stretch up my side. It's dark, a disgusting mixture of purple and blue that makes my stomach coil, my lips pressing together as fresh tears threaten to spill from my eyes. I don't have the option of inspecting myself further. Everett shifts, moving his body so that he can block my reflection, his hand cupping my bruised face.

"They're not going to hurt you again."

My eyes lift to meet his, and although I force myself to nod, I can't bring myself to believe his words.

While I know that *they* can't hurt me again, he can't promise that someone *else* won't. It doesn't seem to matter that I haven't figured out what kind of relationship the brothers and I share—whether I remain their prisoner, or become something more to them, their enemies are coming after me.

I'm never going to be truly free again.

* * * *

Lincoln

"My men are dead." My voice is unsteady as I breathe shakily into the line, my fingers numb around the plastic of the burner in my grasp.

There's a pause, and for once, I wonder if D is caught off guard. He growls, "So get more men! She's a rose among beasts in that goddamn house, and I will not have her tarnished."

"There aren't any other —"

"I don't fund that gang for fucking nothing. Get me more men and bring her home to me. Understand?" He shouts loud enough that the speaker pops in my ear. I wince, shuddering as he takes a steadying breath, unprepared for the words that come next. "And Lincoln? I think it's time we met. You know the place."

He hangs up, his words echoing over the line as the dial tone blares loudly into my ear. Who the hell *is* this guy?

Chapter Twenty-One

Brielle

It's been a long time since anyone has taken care of me. After my mother's devastating cancer diagnosis, she'd been too weak, too sick, and too busy with her chemo treatments to raise a baby, so the responsibility of raising Samuel fell on me. With my father working, I was on my own, feeding him, dressing him, changing him, bathing him...and when my mother inevitably got worse, I found myself doing it all for her, too. It was exhausting, raising a baby, caring for my mother, and going to school. While I was busy worrying night and day about finances, their health, and my grades, I'd managed to lose myself and forget what it was like to have someone care about *me*. I will never regret taking care of them both, but Everett, offering to take care of me, is a change that I find myself welcoming with open arms.

I close my eyes and let out a soft sigh, leaning back into his touch and the gentle caress of his fingers, allowing his presence to ease the anxiety and fear still attempting to strangle me. He's washing my hair, lathering his shampoo through my tangled waves, massaging my tender scalp as he works to remove the blood from my body. There'd been so much of it, coating and sticking to my skin, that the water gathering around the drain by my feet has turned a sickening tinge of red, the sight of it enough to leave me queasy and on edge.

"I'm sorry." I don't know where the whisper of an apology comes from, but I don't shy away from it as it settles into the shower stall with us, nearly drowned out by the sound of water splashing against the tile.

I feel his hands stall in the midst of rinsing my hair, a low growl of disapproval rumbling from his chest. "Don't apologize for this, pet. Caring for you isn't an inconvenience, it's a privilege."

I bite into my lower lip and force myself to nod, unable to control myself from flinching as he presses his lips to my bare shoulder. *I'm sorry.* Those two little words have been spilling from my lips all afternoon, but this time, I manage to force them back. Continuing to say them will only make him feel worse.

I risk a glance at him, my eyes scanning the drenched clothes that cling to his body as he reaches up to grab the bottle of conditioner. After accepting his offer to help me bathe, I'd been surprised when he'd climbed into the shower stall behind me, fully clothed. I don't know how he'd managed to pick up on my unease, and understood my needs without my having to voice them, but I appreciate his thoughtfulness and the comfort his clothed body provides. I'm not sure why, or how to explain it, but his being dressed makes me feel less exposed…even as he works to rid me of the stains left behind by my attackers.

I try to bite back the whimper of pain that bubbles in my throat as he traces a soapy washcloth over my side, but a squeak manages to escape, causing a rough curse to echo from behind me. He takes in a shallow breath as his hands disappear, and a moment later, they return, shifting my body so that my side is underneath the gentle stream as the warm water begins to turn cold.

"Better?" he whispers.

I nod, watching as the hands that had delivered such painful pleasure minutes ago, gently caress my skin and lather me in soap. His eyes skate across my chest, his jaw clenched as he washes my breasts before quickly moving on, his eyebrows furrowing as another low curse hisses through his teeth. I glance down, confused by his reaction, but when I spot the finger-sized bruises beginning to speckle the skin of my chest, I look away, understanding his rage, now.

He trails the cloth across my shoulders again, and down the gully between my breasts, gently lathering my stomach with soap before he drops his hand lower. I jump as he cleans me between my legs, not from fear, but because my body is still sensitive from the orgasm he'd delivered, and he smirks, a knowing smile lighting up his face as he drops the used rag to the floor. He presses a kiss to my forehead as he leans around me to shut off the water, and his steady hands are quick to grab the nearby towel to wrap around me before he gets out of the shower himself. He disappears and returns a few minutes later dressed in fresh clothes, his hands clutching a T-shirt and a pair of boxer briefs for me. I yawn as I dress, wincing as I pull the T-shirt over my head, exhaustion beginning to weigh my body down. Now that the adrenaline has worn off, the lack of sleep from my nightmares is finally starting to take its toll. *I'm exhausted.*

"Come on, pet. Let's get you to bed." Everett's hand wraps around mine, his calloused palm rough against my soft skin as he tugs me from the bathroom and into his room. I try to head for the door, expecting him to take me back to my room, but he pulls me toward his bed instead. He yanks the covers out of the way, and I don't argue or question him as I curl up beneath the sheets. He tucks me in, his fingers softly pushing a wet strand of hair off my cheek. "Sleep well, Brielle."

I fall asleep before the words have left his lips.

Chapter Twenty-Two

Rhys

We live too fucking far from the city.

I growl as I turn onto our empty road, my foot pressing harder into the gas pedal that's already pinned to the floor, my hands tightening on the steering wheel as if doing so will force my car to move *faster*.

Thirty minutes.

It's taken me thirty *fucking* minutes from the time I got Everett's short, uninformative phone call to get home. I've been on edge, my jaw so tense that a headache has begun pounding through my temples as I race toward the gate opening at the end of our drive, the thick metal prying apart just in time for me to drift through the opening. I let off the gas, just enough to make the first curve up the drive, then press down again, the quick, jerky movements of the vehicle causing the bags in my back seat to tumble over. I'd been shopping, attempting to gather enough necessities for Brielle's closet to help her get by, when I should have been *with* her.

I curse as I pull up in front of the house, my shaky hands ripping my keys from the ignition clumsily. My feet thunder against the cement as I race up the front steps, my heart lodged in my throat. *How bad is it?*

I burst through the front door and the momentary surge of anger that rises from the unarmed system is doused out as I spot Dr. Patel, our physician, hovering by the couch.

"Dr. Patel," I call, marching forward with as much composure as I can muster. *What the fuck did they do?* I grip the back of the couch and look down, forcing away the shocked expression that filters across my face when I realize it's *Xander* lying beneath the doctor's steady gaze. Xander *never* gets hurt. "Is he okay?"

"I'm fine," Xander growls, a pained grunt leaving him as Dr. Patel presses a large piece of gauze to a slash that sits just above his left pec. *What the fuck happened?*

His ink-covered skin is decorated in bandages, and a large red stain is beginning to soak into the gray fabric beneath him, proving that he's anything *but* fine. I roll my eyes and raise a brow at the physician, silently asking for his input because I know better than to ask the question again.

"Once I get some fluids into him, he'll be just fine," he replies with a nod, easing some of the worries that have begun to coil my stomach into a tightly wound knot.

I release a long breath, my hands pulling through my waves as I scan Xander's injuries again. "Thank you, Dr. Patel."

There are five different areas on his chest that are covered in white gauze, and while I'm unsure of how many cover his back, I can see from the way that Xander shifts uncomfortably that his already destroyed skin is covered in new wounds. *Who did this?*

"You should be thanking the girl that was with him. He'd be a lot worse off if not for her." Dr. Patel's words filter into the silent living room as he fishes around in the bag lying beside him, a cacophony of questions and emotions crashing down around me as a sickening chill runs down my spine. *Brielle was with him when this happened?*

"Where is she, Xander? Is she hurt?" I ramble, my hands clamping down hard on the couch as I stand, frozen and awaiting his answer. He won't meet my gaze as Dr. Patel starts an I.V., hooking him up to a bag of fluid that hangs from the lamp standing beside the couch. "Xander, where is she?"

"She's in bed." Everett's sudden appearance surprises me, his words tight with the rage I can see brewing within him, his entire body tense.

His jaw is set as he rounds the couch to hover over Xander, and he looks ready to explode, his lips pressed together as his hands bunch into fists at his side. He glances toward the doctor, who's attempting to clean up the mess of bandages on the floor, his arms crossing over his chest.

"Can you give us a few minutes, Doc?" I rub my hand along my jaw, the hair prickling my skin as the doctor nods and makes himself scarce, allowing us the privacy Everett needs to get whatever is drowning him off his chest.

"Tell me they're dead." His hostile words aren't what I was expecting, the venom in his voice jostling me and spurring a new wave of questions as Xander lifts himself into a sitting position, no doubt hating having to lie beneath both our worried gazes.

"They're dead," Xander confirms with a growl, pressing his hand against a square wad of gauze that covers his lower abdomen.

"Can one of you please tell me what the *fuck* is going on? What happened?" I hate being out of the loop and need one of them to catch me up on whatever it was that happened before I lose my ever-loving mind. Everett's brief phone call hadn't given me any information to go on.

"The Wolves attacked them. She pushed him enough for him to take her back, and then this happened." I don't miss the way Everett's voice catches on the word *them*, his head shaking back and forth. "You *have* to fill in the gaps, Xander. What happened? Was Brielle just caught in the crossfire?"

"No." Xander's blue eyes grow cold as he takes in a sharp breath, his large chest tightening as he holds it for a few strained seconds before letting the air slip past his lips again. "When I found her, they had her on her knees in the middle of a clearing. They went after *her*, not me."

I feel like I'm going to be sick, a mixture of nausea and fury souring the food still digesting in my stomach. It's not hard to dissect the meaning behind the unclear picture he's painted for us, and it makes my throat run dry. "Did they—"

"I killed the fucker before he had the chance." Xander interrupts with a rough shake of his head, his black curls spilling around his shoulders from the movement.

"You saved her," I surmise, my words causing his eyes to roll as he swipes his hand across his face and down the length of his beard.

"She shouldn't have needed saving," he mutters, his eyes lifting to meet mine. "There were four of them, but one managed to slip away during the fight."

"Did you get a good look at him?" I ask, knowing that if he *had* seen the man, he'd probably have gone after him, even in this condition.

He shakes his head, his eyebrows furrowing together as he glances down at the array of wounds that decorate his chest. "How's Amour?"

"After a much-needed *distraction* and a shower, she's fine. A little bruised, some broken ribs…but she'll live. I've got her up in my room for now," Everett answers, the hint of a smirk appearing and disappearing on his lips.

A distraction. I know what happened without having to ask, and it drives me to finally draw the line that should've been drawn the moment I realized she was different.

"She's ours, now," I murmur, meeting Xander's gaze.

After everything that's happened, after all the damage he's caused, I refuse to allow him to continue threatening her existence in our home when we're all so obviously falling for her. Xander might be fighting to ignore the attraction that he feels, but after saving her life today, there's no denying that he at least cares about her well-being.

He doesn't argue with me as he nods, his resolve breaking as the walls he'd built to keep Brielle out crumble with his agreement. His eyes dart toward the steps as he lets out a low string of curses, succumbing to the riptide that's already pulled Everett and me under.

"She's ours."

Chapter Twenty-Three

Brielle

Everett's bed is *so* comfortable.

I stretch and burrow my face deeper into his pillow, inhaling his comforting scent as I start to drift back to sleep, unsure of what woke me. It's as the dream is beginning to build behind my closed eyelids I feel it — a quick jab of pain, followed by the loud rumble of my empty stomach. *I'm hungry.* I puff out an annoyed grunt and toss the covers back, my skin prickling with goosebumps as the cool air in the room rushes to surround me, begging me to crawl back under the sheets. I'm tempted, my eyes still heavy with exhaustion, but another loud growl of complaint has me pushing myself to my feet, a cold shiver racing up my spine. *I'm up, I'm up!* I glance around the dimly lit room, the sun that's beginning to set casting long shadows across the ceiling and floor, and gasp as I realize I'm not alone.

"Fuck, Rhys! You scared me," I curse, the air whooshing out of my lungs as a wave of panic constricts them, knocking me back a step.

He's sitting on the floor beside the bedroom door, and while I *know* it's him, his figure too familiar for me to mistake, I can't stop my muddled brain from imagining it's my attackers, coming back from the dead.

"Sorry, Flower...I was actually trying to *keep* that from happening," he apologizes, rubbing the back of his neck. "I didn't want you to be alone when you woke up." His eyes flick across my face, raking over the mess of nail marks and the bruise that must've darkened in color by now, his forced composure cracking as anger flashes in his green gaze. It's gone before I've really had the chance to notice it, a smile plastering across his face again as he pushes himself to his feet. "Why don't we get you something to eat? I can hear your stomach growling from all the way over here."

I hesitate, but only for a moment, my eyes dropping to scan my bare legs before I cross toward him. "Is Xander okay?"

"He's better than he would've been if you hadn't stepped in," he murmurs. He pulls me into his chest, his arms locking around my waist as he presses his nose to my hair, inhaling the mixture of Everett and my scents with a small groan. "I'm glad you're safe, Flower, but I hope Everett tanned your ass. I'm not normally one to deliver punishments, but I have half a mind to bend you over myself."

I squeak, the residual pain left behind by my earlier spanking sparking back to life at his threat, causing a low laugh to rumble from his throat. "What's wrong, Flower? Still sore?"

"Yes." I smile, glancing up at him through my lashes.

He's smirking, his green eyes alight with fire as his hand drops to palm my aching ass cheek, his fingers running over the warmed skin before he squeezes roughly. I hiss, biting into my bottom lip as he releases me, alleviating the pain but leaving me wanting and craving *more*.

"Good." He winks at me and presses a soft kiss to my head, his arm wrapping around my waist as he pulls me toward the bedroom door.

"Can we check on Xander?" I question, my stomach grumbling in annoyance from the roadblock I was putting between it and food.

Rhys laughs, the sound lifting some of the pressure from my chest as he nods and tugs me into the hall. "You don't have to ask permission, Flower, this house is your home now. Why don't you go in there, and I'll order a pizza for us?"

"But—"

"His bark is worse than his bite, trust me," he interrupts with a grin, giving my sore ass a soft tap before tugging out his phone. "Go on, I'll be right behind you."

I nod, my footsteps light against the floor as I creep down the hall, passing my room and another closed door before I come to a stop in front of his bedroom. He was so hostile the last time I attempted to connect with him...so *angry*, and dangerous. He scared me worse than when he'd pressed a gun to my skull, the look in his eye different, darker, feral. *Hateful*. He'd looked at me with *hate*. There's no logical sense in believing that his feelings could have shifted enough to grant me protection and safety from his rage in such a short time, but I can't help but feel like something is different. He's changing, his icy exterior melting. If it weren't, I'm sure I'd already be dead.

I push open his bedroom door slowly, allowing the hinges to announce my arrival. It's dark, the blinds on the windows drawn, the lights off, his large body curled on his side in his bed. *He's asleep.* A small sigh floats past my lips, my hand tightening on the handle as I take a step back to leave, a confusing mixture of disappointment and relief flooding my veins.

"Change your mind?" His tired voice stalls me in the doorway, my breath catching in my throat as my attention snaps back to him.

His blue eyes are searing as he scans me, their intense color reflecting in the light spilling into the room from behind me as his eyebrow raises in question.

"I—I'm sorry, I didn't mean to wake you. I—I just, uh—" I bite my lip, wincing at the awkwardness and uncertainty in my voice. *Why am I so nervous?* Being around him makes my skin crawl with fear *and* excitement.

"Come here, Amour." His surprisingly gentle tone turns the demand into a request, his unrelenting gaze attempting to communicate the plea his pride will never let him say. *Please.*

I swallow the lump in my throat and make my way across the room, fidgeting with the loose string dangling from the hem of my shirt as I stop a few feet from his bed, scanning his injuries. His chest is covered in fresh bandages, some already beginning to speckle with the blood, but that's not what catches my eye. Old scars litter his chest, and while they're nothing compared to the brutal marks decorating his back, they still make my stomach churn with anger. *What kind of torture did this man endure...?*

He shifts, his large muscles contracting as he attempts to force himself up, the pain that flares from the movement causing a loud hiss to escape through his teeth.

"Wait, let me help." I go to support his weight, but freeze when he flinches away, his eyes squeezing shut before he has the chance to catch himself. "Beast…"

"I've got it," he grits out. His nostrils flare with the effort he's exerting to keep himself calm and his jaw is locked and twitching as he shoves a pillow behind his back. Once he has it positioned to his liking, he flicks his eyes open with a grunt and presses his hand to his side, applying pressure, as he settles back against it with a sigh.

"How're you feeling?" I ask tentatively, afraid that the question will spark a thunderstorm of anger I'm not prepared to withstand.

Instead of lashing out, he reaches toward me, his fingers skimming along the bruise encircling my wrist.

"I've been worse," he mumbles, dropping his hand back to his side, his eyes scanning over the clothes that I'm wearing. "How are *you* feeling?"

I hadn't been prepared for him to throw my question back at me, nor had I been prepared for the intensity with which he continues to watch me, his gaze so unmoving it's as if he's afraid I'll disappear.

"I've been worse." I shrug, stealing his words in an attempt to mirror his own aloofness, but, of course, he doesn't accept that answer from me. His chin tilts up in a silent challenge for the truth, and I sigh, my head dropping as my shoulders sag inward. "I'm okay…I— I guess I'm just trying to forget it happened."

"You can try, Amour, but you'll never be able to," he whispers knowingly, a sadness lacing his tone as he drops his gaze to the mess of wounds, old and new, that texturize the ink of his tattoos. He looks…haunted.

I can feel the questions forming in my mouth, the desperate need to understand his coarse personality, an itch that demands to be scratched, but I force the urge away, unwilling to tread any further into the delicate territory I've stumbled into. *I can't push him any further, today.* "I should let you get some rest."

"Hand me those, will you?" He nods toward the nightstand, where two bottles of pills are waiting by an unopened bottle of water, his head dropping back against the headboard. I eye them as I pick them up, scanning their labels before I place them and the water beside his leg, swallowing the new questions his medications spark. "Thanks." The word sounds almost foreign coming from him as he takes a single pill from one of the bottles and swallows it without water, his fingers pressing into his temples as I set everything back on the nightstand beside him. "Goodnight, Amour."

"Goodnight, Beast," I whisper, noting which pill he chose as I backtrack out of the room.

It's as I'm shutting the door that arms wrap around me from behind, a solid chest pressing against my back.

"Scared you off already, huh?" Rhys chuckles, his lips pressing against the side of my neck.

"No, no…I think it actually went okay," I murmur, turning in his arms to look up at him. I bite my lip, contemplating asking the question burning my tongue, but in the end, my curiosity gets the better of me. "How long has Xander been taking sleeping pills?"

His lips press together as if he's not sure whether or not to tell me before he releases a long sigh. "Six months. His nightmares got so bad that he would only sleep for a few hours every couple of days…the pills seemed to help, but he stopped taking them a few weeks ago. I'm glad he's decided to start taking them again."

What happened to him...? The question buzzes around my skull like an angry hornet, demanding to be answered, my heart aching with the pain I can only imagine he's endured. What kind of man could inflict such damage on his own *child*? How did Xander survive?

My breath catches in my throat as the answer to my own question slaps me in the face, fresh tears welling in my eyes as an understanding settles over me and weighs my body down with a sadness that's almost suffocating. He survived...by becoming a *beast.*

Chapter Twenty-Four

Brielle

I bolt upright, the scream that ripped me from sleep still lingering on my tongue. *Where am I?* I heave in a gasp, my eyes whirling around the darkened bedroom, my heart fluttering in my chest as the shadows lining the walls momentarily morph into the shapes of my attackers, my nightmare coming to life. *I'm awake, I'm awake!* I scramble from the bed, a choked cry bleeding through my parted lips as I wobble on my feet, my lungs constricting with the panic flooding through my veins. *I'm awake!*

"Brielle!" a shout comes from down the hallway, but I'm too distraught to respond, my breath coming in short, shallow gasps that leave me lightheaded and unable to speak. *I'm hyperventilating.* "Flower?" Rhys' worried call bursts through the door before he can, his body twisting wildly once he's passed the threshold in search of a nonexistent threat, a gun clutched in his hand. My heart stalls at the sight of the lethal metal, a

188

small whimper rushing from my lungs on the strangled wave of air I'm releasing, the sound forcing Rhys' attention back to me. He flips on the overhead light, his eyes raking over my trembling and sweaty form, his blond brows drawn low over his concerned gaze. "Flower…? What happened?"

I can't explain the fear that's strangling me, or the lifeless shadows that haunt me, can't form the words to explain my nightmare, or how I can still *feel* my attackers' hands on me, as real as the cotton clinging to my curves.

I can't breathe.

I'm suffocating.

He starts toward me, that innate need to comfort others driving him forward, but the loaded weapon in his hand has me clambering away from him until my back smacks into a wall, my eyes squeezing shut. *Breathe, Brielle, breathe!* I double over, my hands clawing at my chest as I pull in short, shallow, unsatisfying gasps, my head spinning like the world beneath my feet. *Am I going to faint?*

"Amour, look at me." Xander's low, calm voice surprises me, the unexpected intrusion of his presence making me jump. I press myself closer to the wall, molding my trembling form against it as I force my eyes open, my blurred vision closing in on the crouched form in front of me. "You need to slow your breathing."

"I—I c-can't," I rasp, the words strangled by my relentless heaving, my legs growing so weak beneath me that I have to lower myself to the ground, my chest and side alight with fire.

"Should I get a bag or something?" Rhys' question floats from across the room, where he's still planted in place, too afraid of my previous reaction to move any closer.

"No, she can do this, can't you, Amour?" Xander replies, his voice filled with support and patience, the mixture so unexpected coming from him that it makes my mind race. "Come back to us, Brielle. Slow, deep breaths."

He demonstrates the breathing technique for me, pulling in long, slow breaths through his nose, before releasing them through his mouth, his bandaged chest expanding with each breath. I try to pace myself, to make my chest move in time with his, but I sputter uselessly, my labored breathing continuing as my heart lurches forward with no intention of slowing down. *I can't do this.*

"You *can,* and you will do this. Keep trying," Xander murmurs, as if able to decipher the uncertainty and disbelief running through my head. He reaches out and grabs my hand, gently pulling it away from my chest so he can press it against his own, wincing slightly before he begins pulling in more slow breaths. I drop my eyes to our hands, watching his chest rise and fall beneath my touch, and use the feeling of his warm skin to ground me as I attempt to match his breathing. I struggle at first, choking on my own panic as I had before, but eventually, with his patience and continued example, I'm able to regain control over my breathing. "Good job, Amour."

I nod at his praise, swallowing the large lump that's formed in my throat. "I—I'm sorry."

I haven't had a panic attack that severe since my mother's death, and now that it's beginning to pass, embarrassment and shame are dropping like heavy weights onto my shoulders.

"No, Flower, don't apologize." Rhys shakes his head, squatting on the floor beside his brother. The gun is gone, either tucked into his pants or stashed away somewhere in the room and while I'm relieved that it's vanished, I can't help wishing the looks of concern plastered on their faces would vanish too. "Do you want us to get out of your hair? You look like you could use a few more hours of sleep."

Sleep? *I don't think I'll ever be able to sleep again.* I shake my head sheepishly, my free hand wiping away the tears still tracking down my face, my eyes scanning the room. While the bright light is helping, I can't stop my gaze from lingering on the dark bathroom, or the sealed closet door, worried that their shadows might shapeshift into the men of my nightmares, too. Xander tugs at my hand, pulling me out of my thoughts, luring my eyes away from the darkness and back to him.

I scan his wounds, injuries he received running to *my* rescue, and pause when I spot the blood beginning to soak through the bandage covering his stab wound, the fluorescent stain too bright to be old. "You're bleeding..."

I instinctively reach toward the bandage, but he flinches away from my hands, his stomach receding as he sucks in a sharp breath, his eyes wide in a momentary lapse of fear. I pause, afraid that I've overstepped, and prepare to retreat, but he lets out a small curse and nods, granting me access to his wound. I take my time pulling back the gauze and wince when I realize that he's torn through a few of his sutures, the stitching broken and unthreading from the skin. *Did he do this rushing in here to check on me?*

"I can probably stitch that back up if you don't want to call Dr. Patel," Rhys offers, catching me by surprise.

I raise a brow at him, watching as he scratches the back of his neck with a large grin. "I had him show me a few easy sutures so we wouldn't have to bother him with menial injuries."

"This isn't a *menial* injury, it's a stab wound. If he's already torn through Dr. Patel's stitches —"

"As long as you don't scream like that again, Amour, his should hold up just fine," Xander interrupts wryly, nodding to Rhys, who's quick to stand and leave.

Xander's watching me, as if his comment didn't just steal the argument forming on my lips or the air from my lungs. *He really is changing, isn't he?* I watch him back skeptically, searching for the malice and annoyance that normally clouds his eyes and features when I'm around, but his eyes are clear, bluer than I've ever seen them.

He smiles at me, *really* smiles, and I'm struck breathless again in wonder. "What's floating through that pretty head of yours, Amour?"

"I—I didn't know..." I trail off, my thoughts evaporating as he shifts closer to me, that beautiful grin still pulling at his lips. *I need to memorize this smile.* He's tentative as he reaches up, his actions uncertain as his fingers brush my cheek, his thumb trailing over my bottom lip before he cups my face.

"You've gotten under my skin, Amour...I'm tired of fighting it, sick of running from the truth," he murmurs, those blue orbs scanning me, tracing my lips, my neck, every inch of skin burning with desire as he leans impossibly closer, his eyes pressing shut.

His lips brush against mine, his beard scratching my chin and his curls brushing my cheek as my own eyes shut, our movements timid and uncertain. I can't help the small moan that slips from me as I press closer to him, my lips parting for him as his tongue snakes into my mouth, exploring me as I straddle his lap. He groans, the guttural sound sparking a surge of desire between my legs as his hands curl in my hair, securing me to him as our mouths blend together in a desperate tangle of teeth and flesh. All the tension, the anger we'd felt for each other, the unspoken desire we'd attempted to bury, melts as we press into one another, unable to get close enough. He grabs my hips, lowering me until I'm pressed against his growing erection, the thin boxers I'm wearing doing nothing to protect my sensitive center as his bulge pokes into me.

"Do you feel what you do to me, Amour? To all of us?" He groans, his lips returning to my skin, trailing along my jaw, across my throat, down the side of my neck, a wicked grin lighting up his eyes. "Do we do the same for you?"

"See for yourself," I whisper, my voice a sultry mix of anticipation and need that turns the dangerous invitation into a demand, my boldness pulling a low growl from Xander's throat. His hand dips underneath the elastic band at my waist and down, his fingers sliding gently across the front of my body until they find the dampness collecting between my thighs.

"Fuck, Amour," he mutters, shifting beneath me as his cock jumps, pressing into me with enough force that a surprised gasp filters through my lips. A pleasurable shiver races up my spine, and he smiles at me triumphantly, rolling his hips up and against me as a knock sounds on the door, snapping our attention back to the forgotten injury in need of our attention.

"Give us a few minutes, Blaze," Xander calls toward the closed door, the protest forming on my tongue evaporating as he slips a finger inside of me. "I'm not ready to share, yet."

I breathe out a moan, chewing on my bottom lip as I fight to stay focused, my eyes darting back toward his bloodied side as he gently moves his finger in and out of my soaking cunt. "Xander...we really should get you taken care of, first."

"Amour, it can—"

"Before you say no," I muse, my voice barely more than a breathy moan, "I have an idea that might make it a little less...interruptive."

He raises a brow at me, a smirk tugging up the corner of his lip as his eyes darken with desire. "And what, Amour, might I ask, is your idea?"

Chapter Twenty-Five

Xander

When did I let her in...?

I'm watching her carefully, my body burning with the desire and need to devour her, and I can't fucking figure it out. When did she melt my icy exterior? When did she break down my walls and slip past the barricades I'd created to protect myself? To keep everyone *out?*

She's leaning over me, one hand stroking the length of my shaft through my sweats while the other keeps her propped up, her eyes jumping between Rhys and me while she waits for one of us to react, unaware that we're both too dumbfounded to respond. I never let *anyone* touch me. There's too much pain associated with physical contact, too much trauma that resurfaces when someone's skin brushes my own... So, why does *her* touch make me feel *alive?* Healed? Whole? Why doesn't it *hurt?*

"You're making it difficult to concentrate, Flower," Rhys grumbles, finally breaking the tension that had stiffened her posture.

She relaxes, her shoulders dropping at his words, and an audible rush of air leaves her lungs as she smiles up at us meekly, her eyes dropping to Rhys' lap and the bulge beginning to tent his shorts. He lifts his green eyes to mine, just long enough for me to sense the warning hidden beneath their heat, before he turns them back to Brielle, a smile pulling onto her lips as she tucks her hand beneath my sweats. *I need to be careful with her.* He chuckles and shakes his head, his biceps twitching with the effort to keep them steady as he threads the first stitch through my side and ties it off, amusement filling his eyes as Brielle freezes beside me.

"Problem, Amour?" I muse, grinning wickedly as her fingers brush the head of my unrestricted cock.

Her eyes widen, and a surprised gasp slips from her lips as she realizes that I've forgone any underwear, but she's quick to compose herself, her head shaking back and forth as she wraps her hand firmly around my shaft and pumps. I jolt, the movement so quick and unexpected that a long moan lashes from the back of my throat, the feeling of her soft skin sliding along my length making my cock harden further in her palm. *Fuck.*

"If this scars, Xander —"

"One more won't kill me," I interrupt with a groan, dropping my head back onto the pillow as she pumps her hand again. *This girl is playing with fucking fire...*

"Can I take these off?" she asks, and although the question is about *my* pants, when I glance down I realize that it's Rhys' response she's waiting for. *One day she'll learn.*

"I think you'd better finish what you started, Flower." Rhys' gravely response makes her shiver, her nipples visibly pebbling beneath her shirt as her eyes lift to meet mine.

She grabs the waistband of my pants and drags them down my legs, her mouth popping open as my cock springs free, a small moan of appreciation escaping her as she studies me. She wets her lips, her tongue dragging slowly along the swollen flesh, but it isn't until she's already leaning toward me that I realize what her idea had been all along.

"Amour, wait." I reach out, my fingers tucking beneath her chin so that I can stop her, mid-descent, my stomach twisting with guilt as her confused and pained eyes meet mine once more. I don't know how to explain my fear to her, a fear that if she attempts to do what those *dogs* wanted to force on her she'll be transported back to that clearing, but I don't want her to feel rejected, either.

"I'm okay, Beast," she whispers. Her eyes are soft with understanding, as if she's somehow able to decipher my concern, an appreciative smile tugging onto her lips. "I know our safe words. If it's too much, I promise I'll use them."

Our safe words? *Everett.*

I slip my hand around the back of her neck and pull her toward me, hungrily pressing my lips to hers as Rhys threads the needle through my skin again. I bite out a groan, my teeth grinding together as she peels herself out of my grasp and slowly re-takes her position by my waist, a timid smile curling her lips.

"Promise you'll finish fixing up his side before you join us?" she whispers across me, the feathery heat of her breath making my thighs clench in anticipation.

"I think I can manage that, Flower, as long as you put on a good show for me," Rhys, ever the voyeur, replies with a smile, shifting closer so he can have an unencumbered view.

She blushes, her cheeks warming with heat as she turns her attention back to my cock, her hand wrapping around my shaft as her tongue darts past her lips. She swipes up my length, her heated eyes meeting mine as her tongue swirls around my head, skimming over the tip to collect the pre-cum that's collected there before her lips close around me.

"Fuck, Amour," I curse, my hips rolling with pleasure as she gently takes me into her mouth. She smiles around me, pleased, as she lowers herself further down my shaft, taking me deeper into her mouth until I can feel myself hitting the back of her throat. I grit out a groan, pain mixing with pleasure as Rhys works to re-suture my wound, my hands tangling in her waves as her mouth slips up and down my cock. "Dammit, Brielle." I fist her hair, restraining it at the base of her skull as her hand begins moving with her head. "Fuck!"

She moans around me, the vibration of her groan making my cock jump as her lips brush the base of my shaft. *Christ.*

"Such a good girl, Flower," Rhys praises, lifting a hand from my side so he can brush a stray strand of hair from her cheek. "You're so fucking beautiful with my brother's cock in your mouth."

She shivers at his praise and strains her jaw open further, pulling me further into her throat, spurred on by his approval. I curse, my body quaking as she holds me deep within her and groans, vibrating and constricting her throat until I'm biting back the urge to come. *Fucking hell.* Slowly, she moves, releasing my cock from her velvety throat as she bobs up and down my length again, her enthusiastic idea proving to distract me from the needle threading through my flesh.

I relax into the bed, a long sigh of satisfaction leaving me as I settle and enjoy the sensation of her tongue stroking my dick. I almost forget we're not alone until I feel her shift below me and glance down to see her free hand fumbling to free Rhys of the shorts restricting him.

"Blaze..." She mumbles around me, finally freeing him as he starts to thread the last stitch. She wraps her hand around his dick and swipes her thumb through the pre-ejaculate collecting at his head, spreading it down his shaft, using it to lubricate him while she continues to suck me off. *What a fucking woman.*

"Done." Rhys exhales, tying off the last knot as Brielle pulls off me, her lips popping from the suction she'd kept around me. "What a good girl, Flower."

She smiles triumphantly as she pants, breathless from suffocating herself with my cock, and sits up, her face flushed with color. I reach toward her and run my thumb along her bottom lip, swiping away the mixture of drool and pre-cum that's collected there.

"I have a plan of my own, Amour," I murmur, and press my thumb into her mouth, groaning as she rolls her tongue along my skin to clean it off. "I'm going to let my brother fuck this pretty mouth—" I pause, watching as her eyebrows rise, anxiously waiting for me to finish while she continues sucking on my thumb. "While I stretch out that tight pussy of yours."

Her eyes roll back as if my words can cause an orgasm of their own, her body quivering as she releases my thumb and pants out a quiet. "Yes."

Yes. Tonight, Brielle Beaumont is *ours.*

Chapter Twenty-Six

Brielle

"I'm going to let my brother fuck this pretty mouth while I stretch out that tight pussy of yours." His dirty words send a tidal wave of desire through me, so powerful I feel like I could combust. *Oh god.*

"Yes." I nod desperately as my sex clenches in anticipation.

I *need* this. I need *them*. Xander shifts beneath me, his hungry gaze traveling up my form as he pushes himself onto his knees, his thick and heavy cock straining toward me. My mouth waters at the sight of the bead collecting on his head, but before I can lean toward him to put it back in my mouth, he presses a hand to my shoulder and gently urges me down against the mattress.

"You've been such a good girl, Amour," Xander muses, slipping his hand between my thighs.

I shiver at his touch, my legs widening for him as he caresses me, his thumb circling my clit over the boxers still covering me.

"She *did* put on a good show for me," Rhys purrs, his breath catching in his throat as my fingers brush the head of his cock. I want him in my mouth *now*.

I wrap a hand around him and slide my fist up and down his length, utterly fascinated as he settles by my head. I never knew they could be so... *big*. I may not be well versed in the subject — although I did see my fair share of the male sex during my clinical rotation — but surely, these men are an exception.

He leans down and presses a soft kiss to my lips, then moves back as Xander tugs the shirt off over my head, their ravenous eyes turning soft as they scan my exposed chest and abdomen. I open my mouth, prepared to ask for my shirt back as a wave of unease begins to crash down around me, but the feeling of lips pressing against my skin causes the words forming on my tongue to evaporate. I glance down, watching as Xander moves between each darkened fingerprint and presses his lips to them, his beard scratching along my skin as he gently nips each of them, claiming them as his own. How can a man with such demons of his own be so soft? So caring and *loving?*

A tear slips from my eyes as his lips trail over my bruised cheek, his thumb quick to swipe the bead of salt away as he studies me.

"Do you need us to stop, Amour?" he whispers, holding my face in his hands.

I shake my head, once again remembering the safe words if I need to use them. "No, please, I want...I *need* this."

He searches my eyes again, his look so intense I feel as if he's searching my very soul for a sign that I'm not ready to do this. When he doesn't find it, he nods and pulls away so he can lower himself down my body, his tongue trailing between the gully of my breasts and down my abdomen. My breath catches, goosebumps breaking across my skin as he comes to an abrupt stop at the boxers keeping me hidden from him, and growls, taking the fabric in his hands and tearing it away from me. I moan, my eyes jumping up to Rhys, who's watching me with a grin, his own hand fisted around his cock as he pumps himself with urgency. I writhe as I feel Xander's tongue drag up my center, my body quivering with need as he dips a finger into my sex and closes his lips around my cunt, stroking me so perfectly I already feel the tsunami of an orgasm beginning to build within me. He curls his finger, slipping in and out of my cunt as his tongue swirls around me, pulling cries of pleasure from my chest as I reach up and desperately tug Rhys down to me. With each stroke of Xander's tongue against me, I roll mine across Rhys, savoring his natural spicy aroma as I pull him into my mouth and suck, hard. He groans, his thighs tensing as another moan climbs up my throat, vibrating his cock in my mouth as Xander slips another finger into me, stretching me in preparation.

"Fuck, Flower," Rhys groans, clearly satisfied with my work.

I, however, don't feel like I'm close enough. I try to scoot up the bed, wanting a better angle, and Xander catches the movement, his mouth pausing along my skin.

"What do you need, Amour?" he whispers, his lips glistening with my desire.

"Closer," I murmur, my face flushing with heat as I struggle to articulate my need. Somehow, he understands.

"Up, Amour, get on your hands and knees," Xander instructs, gently slipping his digits from me as I clamber to follow his directions.

I prop myself up and stare at Rhys through my lashes, smiling at the way he watches me with awe. I take him back into my mouth, already more pleased with this angle as Xander's hand skates over my broken ribs. He traces the bruise there as if committing it to memory before his hand drops between my legs once more.

"Be gentle with her, Beast." I hear Rhys warn through the pleasure, his concern for me driving me to pull him deeper into my throat as Xander lines himself up at my entrance.

Will he fit...?

Xander growls out a breath—of warning or understanding—before he slowly begins sliding into me.

"Oh, f—" I cry out around Rhys, my hips bucking at the new and unfamiliar sensation.

He stretches me, but despite the pain biting through my sex, pleasure is beginning to coil in my stomach as he buries himself deep within me.

"Fuck, Amour." Xander's panting, his hands wrapping around my waist as he slowly begins pulling in and out of me. "You're so goddamn tight."

I moan again, gasping as I begin bobbing my head in time with his thrusts, my eyes crawling up the beautiful body before me so I can lock on Rhys' green orbs. His thumb strokes my cheek, his mouth parting in his ecstasy as he watches Xander fuck me from behind. I take him deep, moaning around him as

Xander picks up the pace, the pain I'd felt when he first claimed my virginity slowly beginning to fade with each delicious thrust of his shaft into my pussy. I bounce against him, needing *more,* as my own pleasure builds, Rhys' hand wrapping through my hair as I choke on his length.

"That's it, Amour, suck my brother's cock like a good fucking girl," Xander praises, his thumb pressing into my clit.

"M-More," I moan, the word almost indecipherable around Rhys, but Xander understands and shoves deeper, his length stroking the bundle of nerves within me while his thumb continues to circle me.

Rhys grunts as I swirl my tongue around him again, pulling him closer and closer to the edge I'm riding as Xander slams into me with enough force to knock the air from my lungs. *Fuck.* I don't hold back the cries of pleasure that ring from me as he fucks me hard and deep, his nails biting into my hips as I pull Rhys into my throat with one final moan.

He growls, his seed spilling down my throat as he thrusts into my mouth, the feeling of both of them filling me, taking me, *claiming* me, knocking me over the edge. An orgasm rips through me, my body quivering as my pussy clenches around Xander, squeezing his erect cock until he jerks within me.

"Fuck!" he cries out, pushing into me with an urgent need, chasing his own release as my body writhes beneath him. I meet his thrusts, panting as I keep Rhys' sated gaze, and shout as Xander withdraws and finishes over the bed with a low moan. "God, Amour, what a good girl."

I pant, breathless as I drop onto the bed beneath their gentle caresses, each man watching me with heated, protective, and appreciative eyes. Xander is smiling, that genuine, rare smile that makes my heart flutter unsteadily in my chest as his hand gently strokes my cheek. "*Magnifique, mon Amour.*"

The words are foreign in my ears, but their meaning rings true as he crawls up the bed to lie beside me, that beautiful smile unfaltering on his lips. If he notices my bemused expression, he doesn't comment, a low chuckle leaving him as Rhys plops onto the bed behind me, and wraps an arm around my waist delicately, securing me to him. We're silent, save for our ragged breathing, and I reminisce in the warmth of their bodies around me, protected, safe, and wanted.

Is this what freedom feels like?

Is this the ending I'd always dreamed of having for myself?

I sigh and feel my eyes fluttering shut, exhaustion tugging them closed. A hand strokes over my cheek, and another caresses my hip, lulling me to sleep with the promise of their presence. Loyalty has been proven and now...I belong with the Grimm Brothers.

Want to see more from this author?
Here's a taster for you to enjoy!

The Cursed Rose:
A Rose in Darkness
Haylynn Downing

Coming 2025

Excerpt

Strangers.

"I left another message for your father...I'm sure he'll be here soon."

I hardly register the woman's words as she hovers in front of me, her pink scrubs too vibrant, too happy a color to belong in a night like tonight. My mother. *Our* mother...

"Do you need anything? I can run down to the cafeteria—"

"No." I interrupt her with a stiff shake of my head, refusing to meet her worried gaze as she glances down at my sleeping brother.

"I'll just be in the hallway if you change your mind," she murmurs, her voice quieter, but still nicer than I deserve. *She doesn't understand.*

"Brielle? Can I speak to you for a moment?" A man's voice draws my attention to the door, and when I look up, I see the officer from earlier standing there, watching me. I glance over at Sammy, nestled in a cocoon of blankets on the gurney in front of me, and force myself onto numb legs. I shuffle toward him, my irritated eyes burning as we enter the brightly lit hallway. People continue around us, those in scrubs oblivious to the uniformed officer in their midst, while the patients in gowns pause for a moment to stare. I feel myself shifting and stall just outside the door as I spot a well-dressed woman waiting nearby. Her hair is pulled back into a neat bun at the base of her skull, and she's wearing a dress suit, with a white badge hanging around her neck. I can see the writing from here, big red letters that read "*Children's Protective Services*" with her name, scrawled in black beneath a photo of her. Susan.

"Hi, Brielle, I'm Suzie." She smiles at me, shuffling the stack of papers in her grasp to one arm so she can extend a hand toward me. Sensing my apprehension, she nods at the officer beside her and takes a small step toward me. "I just wanted to ask you a few questions, if that's all right?"

My eyes track around the room before I realize what I'm doing, my body already involuntarily searching the sea of faces for the one I've been waiting for all night. *Nothing.*

Just more and more strangers.

I slowly turn my attention back to the woman, Susan, and nod my agreement with a swallow, knowing that, although she's *asking* to speak with me, I don't really have the option of saying no. She gestures to a set of chairs behind me and moves to make herself comfortable in one of the blue plastic seats, but I hover in front of her, my mind drifting back to Samuel.

"I'll go sit with him," the officer, whose name I've forgotten, offers with a tight smile. Again, I don't have the option of declining. He's quick to disappear into the exam room before I can think of a rebuttal, the faint click of the door shutting, sealing my position out here, with another stranger.

"Why don't you have a seat, Brielle?" Susan smiles up at me, her brown eyes attempting to search mine before I have the chance to drop them to the floor.

"Am...I in trouble?" I whisper, wondering momentarily if being unable to save my mother is punishable by law.

"Why would you be in trouble?" She asks as if my question is absurd.

I shrug, unsure of how else to answer as I lower myself lethargically into the chair beside her. *I'm exhausted.*

"I'm very sorry for your loss."

Again, I don't reply. What am I supposed to say? I'm sure the standard 'it's okay,' or 'it's not your fault' would suffice, but I've been through too much tonight to expend any more energy trying to console *her.*

"How long was your mother ill?"

Was. Past tense, because she's... I wince and swallow around the lump that's formed in my throat. "Two and a half years."

Truthfully, we'd known something was wrong her entire pregnancy, but it wasn't until after Sammy was born that the doctors discovered the mass growing in her skull.

"That's a long time to live with a terminal diagnosis. How did your family cope?" She jots something down in her notebook and returns her expectant gaze to me, her pen poised against the paper as if already predicting my answer worthy of notating.

"W-we just did what we could." I shrug again, unease churning my empty stomach. I'd probably feel nauseous if I hadn't already thrown up everything in my system.

"What about your father? How did he cope?" Her question ignites a surge of anger through my tired brain as if she's just dropped a bomb in my lap, and I become defensive before I even realize where this is going.

"He works a lot to try and pay for her medical bills. What's this about?" I bristle in my chair, pressing my hands together in my lap as I lift my eyes to meet hers.

She sighs and shuffles the papers in her arms, one shoulder rising and falling half-heartedly. "We're just trying to figure out why you were left alone with your three-year-old brother and your severely sick mother… That's a lot of responsibility to place on a child's shoulders."

"I'm seventeen. I'm old enough to be left alone." My rehearsed excuse doesn't seem to sit well with Susan.

She raises a brow at me and looks up from her notes with a quizzical expression. "Do you know where your father is tonight, Brielle?"

"I already told the officers that he's at work. He has to keep his phone silenced while he's on the clock." *Maybe if I say it enough, it'll be true.*

I know he's *not* at work. If he were, the work boots he'd worn out of the house this morning wouldn't be sitting on the closet floor back at home. I don't know where he is, or what possible explanation he can have for leaving late at night, and dodging every single *fucking* phone call.

"Brielle, we called his job site, and they said he was let go a few months ago."

I blink, unsure if I've heard her correctly. *Let go?* "That's impossible," I whisper as my world tips on its axis. *He was fired?* "He's still getting paid, I've watched him cash the checks."

She shifts, her face falling as if it pains her to see my world come apart at its seams. Where is he? Why wasn't he home? He could've helped.

He could've *saved* her.

"Where are my kids? I want to see my kids!" A familiar voice booms from down the hallway, and when I glance up, I can see my father, shouting at the nurse in the too-happy scrubs by the nurse's station. She's flustered, I can see that from here, her face heating as she crosses her arms over her chest.

"Sir, if you have a seat in the waiting room, I'll have someone come and talk to you —"

"No! I need to see my kids. You can't keep them from me!" He's causing a scene, his voice darker than I've heard it, and his face is puffy from crying. He can't see me, tucked around the corner behind an empty gurney, and although I know I should run to him before he makes things worse, I stay planted in my seat. He backs up, moving away from the desk to a tray of unattended medical supplies, and knocks it over, the loud crashing disturbing the otherwise quiet hospital. People have stopped to watch as he shuffles around, and Susan is quick to slip from beside me to grab the officer from Samuel's room.

"Well?" My father is seething, jabbing a finger at the other medical staff who've stopped to listen. "Where the hell are they? Samuel? Brielle? Brielle!"

* * * *

"Brielle." A gentle caress along my arm stirs me from my sleep, the nightmarish memory evaporating with each pass of their fingertips against my skin. "Let's get you under the covers."

I open my eyes enough to see Rhys leaning over me, his gaze warming away the chill that's seeped into my bones as he continues stroking a warm path down my arm. I groan out a weak protest, still exhausted, and furrow my brows as he chuckles and lifts the covers out from beneath my legs, prepared to tuck me in.

"Wait, let me clean her up first." Xander's voice comes from across the room, and it's only now that I realize his gloriously large and naked body is no longer lying beside me. He's standing at the sink in the en suite, his long black curls restrained in a loose ponytail behind his head as his hands work to wring water out of the washcloth in his grasp.

I will never get used to the beauty of these men. I stretch as he crosses toward me, my muscles weak and gelatinous from my climax, and gasp as he runs the warm cloth up my inner thighs, the intrusion making me shiver. He's watching me carefully, his blue gaze intense as he rids me of the stickiness left behind by my arousal, the intimacy of his actions making me flush with embarrassment.

"Amour, are you hurt? You're bleeding."

I glance down as he pulls the cloth away from me, the white now stained with the color of my innocence. I look between the two men, confused. "I-isn't that supposed to happen?"

Xander's face mirrors my own confusion, his eyebrows rising in question before his tanned cheeks begin to pale and his eyes widen in horror.

"You were a virgin...?" His voice is so low I'm not sure if he's truly searching for an answer, the confusion contorting his features quickly morphing into anger as his steely gaze turns on Rhys. "She was a virgin and you knew. You knew?"

"Xander—" I begin to protest, but my words are cut off by the sound of someone shouting, a slew of curse words filling the otherwise silent home beyond my bedroom door. The guys jump, scrambling for their clothes, but I can't move, my body too tense with surprise and fear. "What is that?

"Stay here with Brielle." Xander barks the order over his shoulder as he rips open the door, his body tensing with unease as another pained shout reaches the top of the stairs.

Everett. *Where is Everett?*

I jump from the bed, grasping for the blanket, and wrap it around myself as I dart around Rhys and into the hallway behind Xander.

"Flower, it's not s—" Rhys' words cut short as he reaches me by the railing, the house falling silent as we stare down in confusion at the unconscious and unfamiliar man lying on the floor below us.

Everett is standing over the stranger, huffing, his gun in his grasp as he glares angrily up at his brothers. "Are you going to stand there and stare, or are you going to fucking help me?"

About the Author

A mother, wife, and avid reader, Haylynn Downing grew up with an innate love of writing. In every notebook from her childhood, you can find doodles of characters and stories scribbled amongst the schoolwork that was meant to be on their pages. A resident of the Midwest, Haylynn spends her free time enjoying the ever-changing weather with her family, and creating books for her readers to enjoy. As a newly found erotica reader, it wasn't until 2020 that Haylynn discovered her passion for writing steamy, sexy romances. Now, not a day passes that new plotlines and possessive alpha males aren't taking up residence in the back of her mind, just waiting to come to life.

Haylynn loves to hear from readers. You can find her contact information, website details and author profile page at https://www.firstforromance.com

Home of Erotic Romance

Sign up for our newsletter and find out about all our romance book releases, eBook sales and promotions, sneak peeks and FREE romance books!